CW00530954

A COMPELLING FORCE

It hadn't taken Ivory Weston long to fall in love with Jacob Pendragon. But was the compelling force she felt only on her side, or did Jacob feel it as well?

Books you will enjoy
by MARGARET MAYO

DEVIL'S FANCY

It hadn't been Fiona who had embezzled from Brandon Rivers' firm, but her identical twin sister Faith—but she couldn't manage to convince Brandon of her innocence, and he proceeded to drag her off to the Bahamas to carry out his revenge. And then Fiona realised she was falling in love with him . . .

BRANDED

It was hardly surprising that Latham Elliot should hate her brother Carl, Susi thought ruefully, after the terrible thing that Carl had done to him. But for the same reason it was hardly likely that Latham would think kindly of her, was it—let alone return her love for him?

PERSONAL VENDETTA

It was a sad shock for Holly when she heard of the deaths of her beloved grandparents. She had a much greater shock, though, when she found out how they had died and that the new laird, Calum McEwen, was laying claim to the cottage in the Scottish Highlands where they had spent their lives!

A COMPELLING FORCE

BY
MARGARET MAYO

To Glad → Dave

(Happy Birthday, Glad)

Margaret Mayo

March 1985

MILLS & BOON LIMITED
15–16 BROOK'S MEWS
LONDON W1A 1DR

*First published in Great Britain 1985
by Mills & Boon Limited*

© Margaret Mayo 1985

Australian copyright 1985

ISBN 0 263 10783 3

*Set in Monophoto Plantin 11 on 11 pt.
07–0385 – 53188*

*Made and printed in Great Britain by
Richard Clay (The Chaucer Press) Ltd,
Bungay, Suffolk*

CHAPTER ONE

CORNWALL fascinated Ivory. It was the first time she had holidayed in this beautiful corner of England but she had fallen immediately in love with it. It had a wild magnificence that appealed to her and at this very moment sitting in Jamaica Inn at Bolventor, she tried to recapture the atmosphere that Daphne du Maurier had portrayed so vividly in her novel of that same name.

So deep in thought was she, imagining the terrifying landlord, Joss, and his frightened niece, Mary, that it was a while before it dawned on her that her friends had disappeared.

She knew Debby and Clair would not go back to the caravan without her, but nevertheless she dashed outside to make sure that Clair's car was still there.

So intent was she on finding the blue Mini that she failed to see another car racing through the car park. When she did it was too late. The wing caught her leg a glancing blow, spinning her off balance so that she cavorted backwards and fell heavily on to the flint-like surface of the yard.

Brakes squealed and the next second a giant of a man with a murderous expression berated her for not looking where she was going. From her prostrate position she looked up into cold blue eyes set in an angular, arrogant face. A tough square chin jutted and a wide mouth was drawn into a grim, taut line. He looked very formidable.

'You could have got yourself killed,' he grated.

'Why in thunder's name didn't you look where you were going?'

Ivory rarely lost her temper but this stranger taking her to task for an accident that was entirely his fault made her see red. 'Why did you treat the car park like a race track?' she demanded, trying to push herself up, only to fall back limply when a searing pain shot through her leg. She gritted her teeth and hissed savagely. 'You should have your licence taken from you. You're not safe to be driving.'

An angry frown darkened the man's face, heavy brows knitting, deep furrows grooving the space between them. 'And you, young lady, should use your eyes.' And then on a fractionally softer note. 'Are you hurt?'

'Not so that you'd notice,' she said tightly. 'I just think you might have broken my leg, that's all.'

'Rubbish,' he snarled. 'I hardly touched you.'

Ivory's dark brown, beautifully shaped eyes widened in a characteristic gesture of disbelief, her thick long lashes framing them dramatically. 'Then why am I down here feeling as though my leg's on fire?'

He cursed and dropped to one knee, running exploratory fingers along the length of her injured leg. 'It's all right,' he growled when she demurred, 'I know what I'm doing. Lie still will you!'

Ivory's close-fitting shorts hid little of her long slender legs and although he was looking at her with clinical detachment, as though she was simply a specimen under a microscope, Ivory felt a surprising awareness.

The man had an air of sophistication, of wealth, and an aggressive self-confidence. She felt a strong pull of attraction, that made her heart beat so fast it was frightening, so nerve-destroying that she kicked out at him with her one good leg. 'If you've quite finished, mister, I'd like my leg back.'

Instantly he stood up, looking down at her with an enigmatic expression in his intensely blue eyes. Ivory felt a strange excitement snake through her body, her breathing becoming sharp and shallow.

'You'll live,' he said crisply. 'If you ask me it's nothing more than your feelings that are hurt. Maybe you'll have a bruise, but there's nothing broken. Can I give you a lift?'

At that moment, to Ivory's relief, Debby and Clair came running up, concern on their faces, looking anxiously at the man standing over their friend. 'What's happened?' Debby looked scared.

'Is this your friend?' The big man looked at them down the length of his arrogant nose, and without waiting for their answer said, 'She ran out in front of my car. She's had a lucky escape.'

'I like that,' cried Ivory, pushing her puzzling feelings to one side and hauling herself to her feet using Clair's arm as a lever. 'If you hadn't been speeding——'

'And if you had looked where you were going,' he cut in abruptly, 'you might have saved us both a great deal of inconvenience.'

'I'm sorry, Mr—er?' began Clair.

'Pendragon,' he supplied tersely.

'I'm sorry, Mr Pendragon, if my friend has held you up. You can go now, we'll look after her.'

'Sorry be damned,' snapped Ivory through gritted teeth, the knowledge that she found this hateful man attractive making her angry. 'It was his fault, and he jolly well knows it.'

A pulse jerked in the smooth tanned jaw and he took Debby to one side, saying a few softly spoken words which Ivory was unable to catch. Then without a further glance in her direction he jumped into his sickly yellow sports car and drove away.

This time he moved slowly over the car park but once on the open road the engine raced and he disappeared before they could bat an eyelid.

'Phew!' exclaimed Debby. 'Some man, that. What did he say his name was, Pendragon? How unusual!'

'How apt,' snarled Ivory. 'Can't you see him breathing fire? I've never met such a hateful man in all my life. Hell, my leg's killing me. Help me to your car, Clair. I must sit down.'

All the way back to the caravan site at Newquay Debby and Clair did nothing but talk of the man who had knocked Ivory down. She herself sat in pained silence, wondering at the feelings he had managed to evoke. Never had she reacted so strongly to any man. Even now she felt a tingling awareness where his long well-shaped fingers had touched her leg and even though he had been angry, she was sure that he, too, had experienced a similar sort of response. For one second there had been something in his eyes which suggested that he found her attractive, then it had gone. Perhaps she had imagined it— or perhaps, even worse, it had been wishful thinking. There was no chance, anyway, that she would ever see him again. It was best to push him right out of her mind.

'Can't you shut up about him?' she cried angrily, after listening to their incessant chatter for as long as she could take it. 'You wouldn't be so enthusiastic if you'd been on the receiving end of his sharp tongue, or if you'd been whacked on your leg by his car.'

Her two friends looked at each other with wide expressive eyes, then Debby turned to her. 'You're crazy. He's the sexiest man I've ever seen. He couldn't help knocking you down, I'm quite sure. He really was most concerned.'

'Huh!' said Ivory disgruntledly. 'He's callous and unfeeling and if he's the sort of person Cornwall breeds then I don't think I'll be paying it a second visit.'

Her friends clearly did not share her opinion, but Ivory had no intention of revealing that he had affected her as much as he had them. He was different from any other man she had ever met. There was an aura of sensuality about him that was impossible to dismiss. He disturbed her peace of mind in a way that was not good for her and she was glad she would never see him again.

A couple of days later Ivory had nothing more than an immense technicoloured bruise and a certain amount of soreness to remind her of her accident. But when Clair and Debby announced they were going horse-riding she opted out. 'I'll stay here,' she said. 'I don't mind, really I don't. I'll go for a swim.'

The two girls did not need much persuading and Ivory was glad. It made her feel guilty to think that she was spoiling their holiday. It had been stupid to rush out as she had, not that she would ever have admitted that to Mr Pendragon. The fact that he had hit her had been as much his fault as hers. As a driver he should have looked where he was going.

She had thought about him a lot over these last two days and had decided that her reaction to him had been stupid and unworthy. He was a hateful man. He had treated her abominably, saying that the accident was all her fault. And most probably he was married anyway!

She picked up a towel and limped down the caravan steps. A car pulled up sharply in front of her and she felt her pulses race. There could not be two cars of that unmistakable shade. But what the hell was he doing here?

He heaved himself out, straightening his long muscular limbs with slow fluid movements which gave him an animal grace, reviving all of Ivory's feelings which she had done her best to squash.

Nevertheless she was determined not to let him see that he in any way affected her. She tilted her head belligerently, waiting for him to speak. Her long dark hair hung heavily against her slim bare shoulders. Her white and red polka-dot bikini complemented the honey-gold tan she had acquired during the last few days.

For the moment the towel hid her bruise from his probing gaze and she looked what she was; a young healthy girl, full of vitality, energy and unconscious grace, with a glowing skin and bright clear eyes. Many times she had been told she ought to be a model, but although she had a keen interest in clothes it was her own boutique she wished for more than anything else. Money was the only thing that was stopping her, plus the fact that at the moment she was busy gaining experience working in a very successful and very busy boutique in London.

'You've suffered no ill-effects, I see?' He wore tight faded denims that hugged his long powerful legs, and a red sleeveless tee-shirt which revealed a deeply bronzed muscular chest and tough sinewy arms. Ivory had difficulty in dragging her eyes away.

He raked long fingers through his strong shiny black hair, trying to tame it into some semblance of order after his no doubt hairy dash through the Cornish countryside. It made no difference, it sprang back into tousled disorder. He might as well have left it alone.

'I'm okay,' she replied, aware that she sounded oddly breathless—and was it any wonder when this perfect physical specimen of masculinity appraised her with insolent intimacy. 'Why are you here?'

'To reassure myself that our, er—skirmish, had no unfortunate consequences.' His remarkably vivid blue eyes did not miss one inch of her slender body, beginning with the perfect oval of her face with her expressive dark eyes, her high cheek bones and soft delicate outline of lips that were neither too generous nor too thin.

He followed the slim column of her throat, over the thin strip of material, across the flatness of her stomach and the gentle roundness of her hips, and down the tanned length of her slender legs, finally finishing with her pink-painted toe nails.

Ivory felt colour flare in her cheeks. She had never before had anything to do with this type of man. She did not quite know how to take him. All she knew was that her body responded dangerously to his. 'I'm fine,' she managed huskily. 'How did you know where to find me?'

He smiled, and she was amazed at the difference it made to his face. His teeth were white and even and the slight hollows in his cheeks filled out. He lost some of his aggressiveness, although there was no mistaking that self-assurance, that confidence that came from being in authority. He might be dressed in the

most casual of clothes but he was without doubt a
man who had made his mark in life, a man who
commanded and expected respect. 'Your friend
told me.'

Ivory shivered at the raw sensuality in his
voice, and wished she had asked Debby what he
had said to her. It would at least have prepared
her for this totally unexpected visit. 'Now you
know,' she said in an odd squeaky little voice,
that sounded nothing like her own, 'you can go.'

He looked at the towel in her hand. 'You're
going swimming, I see? I've half a mind to join
you.'

The very thought brought a surge of blood to
Ivory's head. 'You can't,' she said quickly, too
quickly. 'It's a private pool. It belongs to the
camp site.' The very thought of him keeping her
company for the next hour or so was enough to
send her dizzy with delight. But it was
dangerous, far too dangerous. She had the
strangest feeling that anything she had to do with
this man spelt disaster.

Airily he lifted his broad shoulders. 'I'm sure
no one will stop me, not if you explain I'm your
guest. I caught a glimpse of it on the way in. It's
empty, simply asking to be used.'

Before she could respond he peeled off his tee-
shirt and began unbuckling a wide leather belt.

Ivory turned away in swift confusion and
glanced covertly about to make sure no one was
watching this uninhibited display. One thing was
clear, when this man made up his mind to do
something he did it. She guessed no one was ever
able to stop him.

'Don't be shy,' he said softly. 'I do have my
swimming trunks on. I'm quite decent.'

There was amusement in his eyes when she

turned around and she dropped her lids quickly, then wished she hadn't when her attention was drawn to the superb fitness of his body. There was the merest scattering of dark hairs on his muscled chest, his stomach was flat and hard, his slim hips were covered by the briefest of black trunks, and his legs were long and powerful. His tan was definitely not one that he had acquired in this country. It would take more than an English summer sun to produce that rich copper shade.

One word sprang to mind—virility! It was not a word she normally used, nor even associated with any of the boys she knocked around with. But Mr Pendragon was not a boy—he was a man. And some man! Certainly far more sophisticated and worldly-wise than any of her friends.

It made her wonder why he was taking an interest. She must seem but a child to him. 'Do you know how old I am?' she asked abruptly. Her thick lashes framed her velvet brown eyes as she glanced up at him. She looked very innocent and very young and his eyes narrowed as if wondering what she was getting at.

He lifted his wide shoulders in a careless shrug. 'It's difficult to tell with girls these days. Is it important?'

'I'm eighteen, just,' she said tightly, 'and you must be over thirty. What are people going to think, seeing us together?'

He grinned. 'That I'm lucky to be entertaining a beautiful young girl like you? I'm almost glad you did run in front of my car, otherwise we would never have met.'

There was a warmth in his eyes that had not been there the first time they met and Ivory had the sudden feeling that she was out of her depth.

'I wish we hadn't,' she said quietly, relieved he could not see the sensations which were racing like quicksilver through her nerves.

'Why?'

The abrupt question startled her and her eyelashes fluttered upwards in an unconsciously provocative gesture. She ran the tip of her tongue over her lips and wished she did not feel as though she was about to suffocate. 'You—you're not my type,' she husked. Unfortunately, she added to herself. 'I really don't know why you've come here today. There was no need.'

With a dramatic gesture he placed a hand over his heart. 'My conscience bothered me. I simply had to make sure there were no after-effects.'

She smiled weakly and he laughed. 'Come on, my little beauty. The water's waiting.' He plucked a towel from the back of his seat and Ivory wondered whether he was always so well prepared, or whether he had decided in advance exactly what he was going to do today. She imagined he had. He was that type of man.

She fell into step beside him, vitally aware of his extraordinary sensuality, her breathing so much quicker than it ought to have been. Her head only reached as far as his chin and she was forced to give an occasional skip to keep up with his giant strides. It was all like something out of a dream.

It was not until they reached the water's edge and she dropped her towel on to the grassy bank surrounding the pool that he noticed her bruise. At first he looked distinctly shocked, then anger took its place. 'Did I do that?'

The harsh ejaculation startled her and she bit her lower lip, surveying him anxiously as she nodded.

'Hell! I never realised. Have you seen a doctor?'

Ivory shook her head, feeling warmed by his concern. 'It doesn't hurt now, not much anyway, and like you said it was my own fault.' Now why had she said that? Was she going soft? He had done this to her. This big man—who had the ability both to annoy and charm. She ought to hate him. She told herself she did. She had believed it until he turned up here again today. Now she was torn two ways, trying hard to ignore the emotions which were churning her stomach, but aware that these were some of the most beautiful feelings she had ever experienced. There was no way to describe the heady excitement created by this man's nearness.

He took her arms gently. 'My dear girl, if I'd known, I'd have never let you go so casually. Are you sure it's not troubling you?'

Ivory gave a weak smile and wondered if he could hear the erratic beat of her heart. 'I'm hardly aware of it,' she whispered. She was aware of nothing except him. Her surroundings blurred until she could see only the lean well-defined face, those hooded blue eyes looking at her with such tender concern that she thought she was going to faint. Things like this only happened in films.

'Yet it's kept you here while your friends have gone out?'

'How did you know?' A tiny frown creased the porcelain smoothness of her brow.

'I saw them.' His eyes never left her face.

'Did they see you?'

'I don't think so.'

'They were going riding,' she offered quietly. 'I thought it might be a bit too much for me. I didn't want to risk a fall and maybe hurt my leg some more.'

He nodded grimly. 'A sensible decision. Are you up to swimming?'

She smiled. 'I wouldn't attempt it if I wasn't. Actually the water helps.'

He relaxed and grinned with unexpected boyish enthusiasm, which looked odd on his faintly world-weary face. 'Then why are we waiting?'

Ivory had known instinctively that he would be a good swimmer. He was the type who would be good at anything he set out to do. But she was an excellent swimmer herself and thoroughly enjoyed racing him up and down the length of the pool.

The camp was unusually deserted this morning—and she was grateful, because she did not want to share these precious moments with anyone else. Exactly why he had decided to give up some of his time and spend it with her she did not know. She was sure there must be other things he would much rather be doing. But whatever the reason she was enjoying herself in a very different way from anything she had done before.

At length, breathless and exhilarated she hauled herself out and flopped down on to her towel. A hot summer sun burned down from a cloudless blue sky. It was a perfect day.

He lay beside her, leaning on one elbow, eyeing her with lazy speculation. 'Quite a little performer, aren't you? Do you throw yourself into everything you do with such vigour?'

'I enjoy swimming,' she said simply, and because there was an expression on his face that caused utter confusion inside her she closed her eyes. Even so it was impossible to shut out her awareness of him. Something told her that he found her desirable too, and she was not quite sure that she knew how to deal with it.

When she felt him smooth back a stray strand of hair from her face her eyes shot open and she jerked away. Although quite an ordinary gesture there had been something intimate in the way he did it. His fingers had lingered unnecessarily long on her face, burning her skin, making her vividly aware that he was no beginner when it came to the art of arousing a girl's emotions. It occurred to her that there was more to his being here than simply concern over her health. Maybe he was after an affair! And heady though the thought was—it was definitely not on.

He put a gentle finger beneath her chin and turned her head back towards him. 'Are you afraid of me, little girl with no name?'

Involuntarily the beginnings of a smile lifted the corners of her mouth. 'It's Ivory,' she said softly. 'Ivory Weston, and no, I'm not afraid, but you're too old for me. You can be after only one thing.'

Only a flicker of his eyelashes suggested that her insult had hurt. His voice when he spoke was still amused. 'I expect all your boyfriends have been seventeen and eighteen year olds? Totally inexperienced when it comes to knowing what a woman wants?'

Ivory moistened her lips and felt herself grow warm. Suddenly she wished they were surrounded by people. Things were threatening to get out of hand. 'I'm not a woman.'

'You have a woman's body,' he said softly, his eyes dwelling for a moment on the proud thrust of her breasts, 'and surely you must have a woman's desires?'

Most certainly she had. Erotic emotions such as she had never experienced before raced through her unceasingly. She had every reason to be afraid, not only of this man but herself. How many times had her aunt drummed into her how easy it was to let your physical emotions carry you away.

Nevertheless her eyes locked into his and when his thumb began to stroke the delicate skin of her throat, each movement deliberately sensual, she lowered her lids, her long dark lashes fanning her cheeks.

Shivers ran down her spine and it was all she could do to stop herself from trembling. This was bliss in the extreme.

But when his fingers moved lower, resting first of all on the base of her throat where a tell-tale pulse flickered alarmingly, and then with incredible gentleness began to caress the soft swell of her breasts she reacted violently, slapping his hand away with a swift angry movement. 'How dare you?' she cried. 'What do you think you're doing?'

Unperturbed he smiled. 'Testing your reaction. Trying to discover whether you are immune to an *old* man like me.'

'I'm not immune, Mr Pendragon, but I do object to being mauled by a total stranger.' She sat up, hugging her knees to her chest, eyeing him coldly, even though inside she felt on fire. She had not wanted to stop him, only an inbred sense of what was right and what was wrong making her react as she had.

His eyes glittered. 'So how do you suggest we become better acquainted?'

'Who's saying I want to?' she demanded, trying to look hostile, but fearing she was failing dismally. Never in her life had she felt such a powerful attraction and it was taking every bit of her strength to fight him off.

'Your body,' he suggested insolently. 'It's a total giveaway.'

And of course he was expert enough to realise it! He must have had dozens of women in his life—and she guessed none of them had had the self-control to turn him down. She rather wished she had let him have his way. It was what she wanted. 'I think it is time you went, Mr Pendragon,' she said tightly. If he didn't, if he tried again, she would not have the strength to resist.

'Jacob, please,' he said, ignoring her request. 'You can't go on calling me Mr Pendragon if we're to be friends.'

'We're not,' she said. 'When are you going?'

His lips pulled down wryly at the corners. 'You certainly don't believe in being tactful.'

'I don't like people forcing their attention on me.'

'Was I?' he asked. 'Won't you admit that you quite enjoyed me touching you? But it won't happen again, I promise. Not unless you give your permission.'

He was mocking her again. She glared. 'I still want you to go.' Her heart pounded like a sledge hammer and she was afraid.

'Only if you promise to have dinner with me this evening.'

She shook her head violently. 'I can't. I'm going out with my friends.' It appalled her to think that deep inside she would have preferred to dine with this man. What was it about him that made her react like this?

'Tomorrow then?'

'Tomorrow we go home. I'm sorry, I really would have liked to come out with you Mr Pendragon—Jacob, but that's the way it is.' The knowledge that there was now no chance that she would see him again gave her confidence, even though deep inside she felt dismayed. 'Thank you for coming to see how I was. It was very kind of you.'

The thick brows rose smoothly. 'You're not getting rid of me as easily as that, young Ivory. I'm sure it will be another hour at least before your friends return. I'll keep you company.'

'Why?' she demanded. 'You won't get anywhere with me, if that's all you're after. I'm not that type of girl.'

'I'm glad to hear it,' he said surprisingly. 'There's far too much promiscuity in the world today.' He lay back and tucked his hands beneath his head, closing his eyes against the blazing sun.

Ivory took the opportunity to study his face. His lashes were thick and vital like the rest of him, and there was a web of fine lines beneath his eyes. His mouth was firm and well shaped, his nostrils slightly flared, and there was a hint of shadow on his jaw that told her he was a man who probably needed to shave twice a day.

She felt heady and her breathing came in short gasps and she wondered again that he should take such an interest in her. 'Are you married?' she asked, without even realising that she had said it. It was not possible that a man like him should still be single.

His eyes flickered open and he smiled. Hot embarrassed colour washed Ivory's face as he caught her looking at him. 'No!' That one simple word was all he said before he lowered his lashes again.

'It's men like you who get girls a bad name,' she said.

This time he sat up. 'We do? How do you make that out?' He did not look annoyed by her blunt speaking, merely amused.

Ivory quelled a shudder motivated by the sheer primitive maleness of this man, but did not deviate from her track. 'How many girls turn you down?'

'Not many,' he admitted. 'In fact I would say that you are the first one.'

'There you are, you see,' she pounced. 'You're the reason girls are promiscuous. Men are to blame, not women. If you didn't try it on——'

He put his hand over her mouth. 'It's yourself you're trying to convince, Ivory, not me.'

She shook herself free. 'Then why aren't you married?' she shot. 'I'll tell you why, it's because you've always got what you wanted without any of the trappings. You don't really want to see me again. It's just that you're peeved because I'm not like the rest. You thought you'd try again, that's it, isn't it?'

Ivory hadn't a clue why she was rabbiting on like this, unless it was because her security was threatened. She had always known where she was going. For years she had had one plan in mind—to open her own shop. Lord knows why she felt this man was a danger to her future—but she did. It was an instinctive feeling, nothing more, but sufficient to make her feel scared.

'I want to see you again because I—like you.' His eyes searched her face with an intimacy that suggested he was trying to commit it to memory. 'You're different, Ivory. I sensed that the day I unforgivably knocked you down. Where do you live? Perhaps we could arrange to meet some time in the future.'

He sounded sincere and Ivory experienced a flutter of uncertainty. But she was sure no good could come out of seeing too much of this man.

'Surrey,' she said, intentionally vague.

'And who do you live with?'

'My aunt. She brought me up after my parents were killed in a car accident. But it's no good you asking all these questions. I have no intention of seeing you again.'

'Are you still insisting that I'm not your type?' He touched her hair gently. 'There's no such thing. It's chemistry that attracts two people in the first place. And we have that, I assure you.'

His charming smile made Ivory's pulses race, but she shook her head valiantly. 'Your world is not mine, Jacob.'

The tension between them crackled as he continued to stroke her hair. 'We neither of us know anything about each other. How can you say that?'

She lifted her shoulders in a vague little shrug. 'You have money. I'd have to be blind not to know that. It's all about you. You have that air of success—and I'm, well, not long out of school. With ambition, admittedly, but not yet in a position to do anything about it.'

'And for that reason you refuse to see me again?' He looked distinctly disappointed.

'I'm afraid so.' She looked at him candidly, her beautiful wide eyes taking in the handsome lines of his face, the unusual blueness of his eyes, knowing they would be etched in her mind for ever.

'I could help you, if it's money you need.'

Ivory shot away from him angrily. 'And then I'd be in your debt forever? A good way of getting me into bed with you. No, thank you, Mr

Pendragon. Whatever I do will be by my own efforts.'

He frowned, his face becoming once again all hard and uncompromising. 'I was thinking of a strict business deal. I wouldn't insult you by blackmailing you into a relationship you clearly do not want.'

'And how would I pay you back?' she demanded heatedly. 'It would be years before I'd be in a position to do that.'

He shrugged carelessly. 'That wouldn't worry me.'

'It would me,' she cried. 'I suppose I should thank you for your generous offer, considering I'm a stranger, unless you were thinking of it as compensation for the injury you caused me? But whatever, it's not on. Please go, Mr Pendragon. I don't want to see you again.'

'You mean that?' The blue of his eyes darkened dramatically, and he looked absurdly disappointed.

She nodded, swallowing a sudden constricting lump in her throat. It was not what she wanted at all but it was ridiculous feeling like this about a man she had just met—a man almost old enough to be her father!

'There is nothing I can say that will make you change your mind?'

Not trusting herself to speak she shook her head.

With a savage gesture he pushed himself up and strode away, and although Ivory desperately wanted to call him back she knew it was for the best. No man offered money to a person he had just met, especially a girl of her age, unless he had some ulterior motive. The thought sickened her and she struggled to her feet, hugging the

towel about her shoulders and heading for the
caravan the long way round.

By the time she got there his car had gone. She
let herself in and sank down on one of the long
upholstered seats with a curious feeling of relief
and disappointment. He was by far the sexiest
man she had ever met—he could also have helped
her buy the boutique she so desperately wanted.
And she had let him go! Just like that. Wait till
she told Debby and Clair. They would call her all
sorts of a fool.

But she did not tell them. For some reason she
could not understand she kept the news of his
visit to herself. Jacob Pendragon belonged to a
tiny private compartment inside her, to be taken
out and mused over only when she was alone.

She was never able to fathom exactly why he
had chosen to see her again. She could not accept
that he had simply wanted to reassure himself
that she was all right. She was convinced, though,
that she had done the right thing in sending him
away, even if merely thinking about him sent her
senses reeling. There was something very compelling about him, but he was far too old and
experienced for her to be safe.

A few weeks after her holiday he had slipped into
the back of her mind. She could not forget him
completely, he was not that sort of man, but she was
able to submerge herself in her work completely
and not think of him for many hours of the day.

She was kept busy learning the way the
business was run. Ivory had a flair for fashion
and was quick to pick up all that she was told.
Mrs Trussell who owned the shop had taken an
immediate liking to Ivory, and was training her to
take over whenever she was away.

Sometimes Ivory felt guilty because she was using this woman's experience to further her own cause, but would much rather be gaining practical experience like this, and earning a wage, than going through college and learning all about retailing the academic way.

One evening when she was late getting home from the shop it was a distinct shock to be told by her aunt that she had a visitor. There had been a strange car outside, a BMW, shrieking affluence, but as they had no rich friends she had assumed it was someone visiting a neighbour. Her aunt looked flustered, which was unusual for her, and Ivory could not imagine who it might be.

When she walked into the sitting room and saw Jacob Pendragon it was the biggest shock of her life. 'Jacob!' she said faintly. 'What are you doing here?' More to the point, how had he discovered where she lived?

'I came to see how you are,' he said with an innocence that did not deceive her. 'I've been telling your aunt how we met. It appears you never mentioned it.'

She had forgotten how good looking he was, and now her heart did an alarming tattoo. 'Didn't I, Aunt?' she enquired, knowing full well that she had deliberately refrained from mentioning this disturbing stranger.

Her Aunt Eleanor, although very good to her, was not the sort of person she could confide in. She had been widowed at the age of twenty-two and never remarried, and although she had given Ivory a home six years ago she had little knowledge of the way a young girl's mind worked. If Ivory had told her about Jacob she would have been appalled, especially if she had learned how intimately he had touched her.

'Mr Pendragon has been telling me how badly he felt about the whole thing,' said Eleanor, sitting on the edge of her seat and positively beaming at their visitor. 'He said he's not been able to push it out of his mind. What made him drive so fast on a car park he can't possibly imagine. He said it's certainly made him more careful.'

Who was he trying to kid? Ivory eyed him sceptically and decided that he looked even more devastating in a conventional grey suit than he had half naked. His physical strength was hidden but he still exuded an aura of power and dynamism, of instant sexuality, and a tremor ran through each and every one of her limbs.

It was an effort to smile as though nothing was wrong. 'How nice of you, Jacob. I never expected to see you again. I thought you would have forgotten all about me.'

His returning smile was warm and enveloping. 'I never forget a pretty face. As I was saying to your dear aunt I really have had you on my conscience. How is the leg? Better, I hope. To think I might have killed you. It really doesn't bear thinking about.'

Ivory did her best not to laugh. He was laying it on good and thick and it sounded so funny coming from him. She recalled how angry he had been when the accident happened. How he had lain all the blame on her.

'It's quite better,' she managed to say levelly. 'Not even a mark to show for it.'

'I'm so relieved.' He glanced from her to her aunt. 'I wonder, Eleanor, whether you would permit me to take your niece out to dinner this evening? It is the least I can do to make up for the pain I caused.'

Eleanor! He had certainly lost no time. But then he had not been hesitant in getting to know herself. He was certainly a fast worker when it came to something he wanted. Did it mean he was still attracted to her? Had he come all this way on the off-chance of seeing her again? The thought set her pulses racing and she wondered whether she had misjudged him.

Her aunt smiled warmly. 'But, of course, Jacob. I know Ivory will be perfectly safe in your hands. One has to be so careful these days. There's so much violence in the world.'

'Perfectly true,' he agreed seriously. 'But Ivory's a sensible girl. I asked her out when she was on holiday and she wouldn't come. You've obviously instilled a lot of good sense into her.'

The tall thin woman visibly preened herself. 'I do my best, and I'm glad to hear Ivory heeded my warnings. I feel so responsible for her since my sister died. Run along, dear, and get changed. Another cup of tea, Jacob?'

'I haven't said yet that I want to go.' Ivory's voice was clear and determined. They were both taking her acceptance very much for granted and it irritated her. Although the thought of an evening out with Jacob was exciting, it was also frightening. She knew that he had the power to make her say and do things that were entirely alien to her nature.

She looked at him aggressively, taking in the expensive mohair suit and striped shirt, the gold cufflinks that were discreet enough to have cost a fortune, the sovereign ring, and shoes that had certainly not come from some high street shop. What was it he wanted?

He smiled at her easily and her heart did a peculiar flip. 'But you will come,' he said assuredly. 'I refuse to take no for an answer.'

'Of course she will,' said her aunt. 'It's very childish to refuse, Ivory. Jacob is clearly prepared to give up some of his valuable time to take you out. It's unthinkable you should not accept.'

A hint of a smile curved the corners of his mouth, his blue eyes filled with amusement. 'In the face of such opposition, my injured little friend, you have no choice.'

◀

CHAPTER TWO

IVORY wore a bronze velvet suit for her dinner-date with Jacob, one she had bought from the boutique just the other day. She teamed it with a cream lace blouse and made up her face expertly, fastening her hair in a cluster of curls at her nape, adding gold hoop earrings to her ears. She looked much older than her eighteen years and was very pleased with the effect.

Jacob said nothing when she came downstairs but she could tell by the expression on his face that he approved. Sitting next to him in his expensive car she was again filled with an awareness that was impossible to keep at bay. He threatened her sanity, this big man with the long virile body and the deep sexy voice. He was having his own way with her whether she wished it or not. Getting her aunt on his side had been a stroke of genius.

'How did you find me?' she asked, and was amazed to hear how shaky her voice sounded.

He glanced across and gave her a grave all-encompassing smile. 'Where there's a will there's a way, or so the saying goes. The camp-site manager was more than willing to let me know whose name the caravan was booked in, and your friend, Debby, was delighted to give me your address. I think she smelled romance in the air.'

'Wait till I see her,' said Ivory tightly, but was not really annoyed. She would have been disappointed had she never seen Jacob again.

He took her to an unobtrusively elegant

restaurant where the head waiter fussed over them like a mother hen.

Once they were seated and their drinks and meal ordered Jacob handed her a slim parcel. Ivory looked at it enquiringly and then pushed it back into his hand. 'Whatever it is, no. I don't want to be ungrateful but I can't accept a present from you.'

'Why ever not?' His good humour was not disturbed in the slightest. 'It doesn't mean anything. It's merely a gesture of goodwill—an apology for injuring you, if you like. I shall be very hurt if you don't take it.'

Perhaps it would be churlish to refuse, thought Ivory. In any case, she wanted to know what it was. She sighed and said ungraciously, 'Very well, if it will make you happy. But I can assure you it's not necessary.'

Her fingers shook as she untied the bow of narrow silver ribbon and unwrapped the navy blue paper with a discreet motif that she felt sure must be the trademark of some high-class jeweller. She snapped open the slim leather case and gasped when she saw the dainty gold watch. Shaking her head she thrust it towards him. 'No, Jacob. It's too much. I couldn't.'

'Nonsense.' He looked faintly angry. 'What's in a watch?' He fetched it out of the box and clasped the bracelet around her slender wrist. 'There, it's perfect. If you don't choose to wear it that's your affair, but I don't want it back. It's no use to me.'

Ivory felt that she was being chastised and coloured uncomfortably. 'I didn't mean to be rude, Jacob, it's just that I'm not——'

'Used to accepting presents from gentleman friends?' he finished for her. 'You're so beautiful, Ivory, you deserve to be surrounded by beautiful things. It really was my lucky day when I bumped into you.'

Their drinks arrived and they were silent until he said, 'Tell me about these ambitions of yours. Your aunt informs me that you fancy opening a shop?'

'That's right,' she said, her attention temporarily diverted. 'But she had no right telling you. It's no business of yours.'

'I intend making it my business,' he said, 'but I'm not so sure that I entirely agree with it. You need to be extremely shrewd and hard to make a go of any business, and boutiques are ten a penny. You'd need it to be different from the rest, and also sure that you were on to a good thing. Otherwise you could be heading for disaster. I don't think you're the right sort of person, Ivory.'

She lifted her chin and looked at him angrily. 'Not yet, maybe. This is all in the future. I could kill my aunt for telling you, but since she has I'll put you straight. It will take a long time to save up. By then I shall have a good insight into what is involved and will have become more mature and sophisticated myself. I shall do nothing unless I am very sure and I'd ask you to keep your nose out of my affairs. Buying me this watch doesn't give you any right to interfere.'

'I'm merely giving you advice,' he said. 'Believe me, I do know what I'm talking about.'

'I'm sure you do,' she said coldly, 'but if you intend concentrating on that for the rest of the evening then you might as well take me home. I don't want to discuss my personal life with you.'

'Very well.' As usual he managed not to look in the least put out. 'What would you like to talk about?'

'You perhaps?'

'That wouldn't be fair since you've made yourself a taboo subject,' he remarked smoothly.

Ivory was glad the waiter arrived at that moment with their smoked salmon, and soon her inhibitions were forgotten. She talked and laughed with all the confidence in the world. Jacob made her feel a very desirable woman and she reacted accordingly, not objecting in the slightest when he flirted outrageously, enjoying it even, responding with a coquettishness of her own.

By the end of the evening she felt dizzy with excitement and ached for him to touch her. Each time their eyes met her head spun with desire. It was madness when she knew nothing at all about him, but exhilarating all the same.

When they got back home Eleanor was in bed. Ivory had invited Jacob in, but now she said nervously, 'Perhaps you oughtn't to stay?'

'I'm sure your aunt won't begrudge me a cup of hot chocolate?' He teased her with a smile that turned her blood to water and sent tremors through her veins.

She said, more sharply than she intended, 'So long as that is all you want!' Jacob was far too dangerous a man to tangle with. He knew exactly what he was doing, whereas she had only her heart and her head to guide her.

'My dear virtuous little Ivory,' he mocked. 'I would no more force my attentions upon you than I would upon—your aunt. I made a promise, do you remember?'

The thought of her strait-laced aunt succumbing to Jacob's kisses made her giggle. 'All right, then, but you mustn't stay long. She won't like it, and I have to be up for work in the morning.'

He followed her into the kitchen and spooned chocolate powder into two mugs while she filled the kettle, but although he kept his distance Ivory was as vitally aware of him as if they were embracing.

The atmosphere became claustrophobic and in spite of the fact that she resolutely kept her back to him she knew that he watched her and it became more and more difficult to keep her limbs still. No one had ever told her that it was possible to feel so intoxicated by a man without him even touching her.

Slowly, without being able to help herself, she turned around. Their eyes met and locked with a mind-shattering awareness that coursed through Ivory's limbs like fire, causing her heart to beat like a drum in her ears, exposing every nerve-end to a raw tingling sensuality.

Her breathing grew rapid and shallow and although it could have been no more than a few seconds that they looked at each other, it felt like a life-time. Her breasts rose and fell, her parted lips trembled, and the tension between them was so tangible it shot across the room like a solid object.

When he began to walk slowly towards her, still with those powerful blue eyes locked into hers, there was no way that she could stop him. She even moved a half-step forward and knew that their coming together was inevitable. It had been that way from the moment they met.

His lips brushed hers gently at first, experimentally, questioningly, but when he met no resistance, when all she did was tremble violently in his strong arms, his kiss deepened and he took full possession of her mouth.

The shock to Ivory's system was absolute. The

flood of desire that rushed through her was such as she had never experienced before. It made a mockery of the pleasure she had felt when she had been kissed in the past.

A strangled moan came from deep in her throat as his tongue invaded her mouth with a sexual expertise and she clung to him blindly, half-frightened by her response. No one had ever kissed her like this before. It was a totally new feeling which shot stabs of desire through her body and made her return his kiss with equal fervour.

He moulded her against his muscular hardness, his hands moving over the small of her back, pulling her inexorably closer until she felt as though their bodies were fusing into one.

The kettle boiled but it was not until the kitchen began to fill with steam that Ivory noticed it. Her limbs felt heavy as she pushed herself away, her eyes glazed so that she could hardly see what she was doing.

Jacob made no attempt to detain her, merely watching through half-closed eyes as she filled the mugs. Her hand trembled so much that she spilt water on the table, but at last it was done, and she silently pushed Jacob's across to him.

'I shouldn't have kissed you,' he said quietly.

'I should have stopped you,' returned Ivory with equal remorse.

'It must have meant that you wanted me to kiss you?'

'I did,' she breathed fervently before she could stop herself. 'Oh, Jacob, I did.'

The next moment they were in each other's arms again, kissing hungrily as though they could not get enough of each other. He pulled the pins out of her rich glossy hair, allowing it to fall heavily about her shoulders, running his fingers through its long length, finally shaping her head between his hands and pulling her closer.

His kiss was deep and sweet and Ivory responded in a way that seemed entirely natural, yet was something she had never done before. Against her body his heart beat wild and strong and she was aware of her own rushing away at double-quick time.

Their drinks were forgotten as long minutes passed. His hands moved with slow sensual expertise over her body, exploring each of her perfect curves, cupping her breasts with mind-shattering intimacy so that she moaned and arched herself ever closer towards him.

She lost all sense of time or reason as his mouth left her lips to explore the soft curve of her cheek, to press gentle yet searing kisses on each of her closed eyes, nibbling at her lobes, burning a tantalisingly erotic trail down the slender column of her throat.

Ivory's head fell back in complete surrender, her desire for him taking precedence above all else. The blood roared in her head and she felt they were in a world of their own.

She threaded her fingers through the wiry strength of his hair, exploring the shape of his head, bringing her hands forward to touch his face, feeling the hard bones beneath the firm warm skin.

It was the first time she had ever touched a man in such a manner and the sensations she experienced were enough to drown her in a whirlpool of desire. Not conscious now of her actions she slid her hands beneath the fine material of his jacket, luxuriating in the feel of his tense muscles through the silk of his shirt.

He groaned and crushed her ever harder to him, his kisses desperate now, feverish, possessing her mouth until she felt herself gasping for air. 'This is madness,' he husked painfully, 'but I want you, Ivory. Oh, God, how I want you.'

'Me too,' she whispered shyly, all thoughts of her aunt forgotten. 'I've never felt like this before, Jacob. It's all so new to me, but . . .'

He shook his head and silenced her with a hard finger that shook. He looked in anguish, his eyes glazed, a faint film of perspiration sheening his bronzed skin.

'No, Ivory, no.' He seemed to have difficulty in speaking. 'It would be wrong of me to do this to you.' His words denied the needs of his body. 'You're too young, too innocent, it would be taking advantage.'

'But I want you too, Jacob,' she heard herself plead. 'Is that so very wrong?' How could he stop when he had aroused her to such a pitch that she felt as if she were going to explode?

'Your aunt trusts me,' he said thickly, and with a suddenness that alarmed her swung away, his hands clasped to his head as if it was throbbing with a pain too violent to bear.

She knew exactly how he felt. She was the same way herself. It was all a very new and very beautiful experience and she did not want him to take it away from her. He had started this thing— she wanted him to see it through.

Tentatively she reached out and touched his bowed shoulders. 'Please, Jacob.'

'No!' The harsh guttural sound startled her and he swung round, his face ravaged with pain. 'Drink your chocolate. It's time you were in bed.'

'You can't do this to me,' she protested, appalled to feel the prick of tears at the back of her eyelids.

'What the hell do you think I'm doing to myself?' he demanded. 'I'm human too, Ivory. But at least I've got the good sense to stop before it's too late. Pull yourself together, girl, for goodness' sake, and stop looking at me with those big beautiful eyes. They're enough to drive any man insane.'

When her tears welled she was unable to stop them. Maybe if she had been older she would have been able to control herself. As it was she was too inexperienced to handle her emotions and felt as though she had been pushed out into the cold.

She hunched her shoulders and turned her back on him, allowing the tears to fall freely, sobs wrenching themselves from her as she discovered this was the only way she could relieve her pent-up emotions.

Jacob groaned and moved towards her. She tensed as he took her into his arms, then relaxed and allowed him to soothe her, resting her head on his shoulder, her tears soaking into the thin material of his shirt.

As she became calmer she hated to think how naïve he must think her, and supposed she should be grateful that he had had the strength to put a stop to what had been a very dangerous state of affairs.

It proved how easily a girl could lose her head. If Jacob had not been so honourable and she had become pregnant her aunt would have thrown a fit. She shuddered at the thought of her aunt's reaction and Jacob held her that little bit tighter.

Eventually she found the strength to move away. 'I'm sorry,' she offered weakly. 'You must think me very stupid. It's just that—— '

'Don't say anything,' he cut in softly. 'Your

reaction was very natural, my dear. If you want to blame anyone, blame me. I should have known. I should never have subjected you to such rough treatment. I'm a bastard and I admit it and I'll try not to let it happen again.'

'But I'm going to see you again?' Ivory raised her tear-stained face to his. His answer was somehow important.

'Try stopping me,' he growled gently. 'You're not going to disappear out of my life as suddenly as you tumbled into it.'

Ivory felt suddenly very happy. Her face became radiant as she picked up her almost cold chocolate and drank thirstily. It tasted like nectar. She would never drink a cup of chocolate again without remembering this moment.

The next morning over breakfast Eleanor was anxious to hear how the evening had gone. 'He's such a gentleman,' she enthused. 'Not many men would bother to follow up a little accident like that.'

Ivory smiled dreamily. 'He is nice, isn't he?'

Her aunt looked at her sharply. 'I hope you're not getting any ideas, Ivory. He was just being kind, no more. A man as rich as he is would certainly not waste his time with the likes of you.'

'He bought me this watch.' Ivory flaunted her wrist beneath her aunt's nose. 'Isn't it beautiful?'

Eleanor looked horrified. 'You must give it him back. People will talk. Do you know who he is? He's the owner of the Semar chain of do-it-yourself shops, for a start. He also has interests in most of the big supermarket companies. He's a millionaire many times over and has business connections all over the world. If you accept gifts from him people will think you're ...' She stopped, embarrassed.

'His latest lover?' enquired Ivory pertly. 'Don't worry, I know exactly where I stand—and I did try to give him the watch back, but he was most insistent.'

'Are you seeing him again?' enquired her aunt sharply.

Ivory shrugged. 'I've no idea. He didn't say.'

'It wouldn't be wise. He has a reputation, Ivory, for dating the world's most beautiful women—very rich women, I might add. You're not in their class, I'm afraid. He was just being kind so far as you were concerned. The best thing you can do is push him right out of your head.'

'I expect you're right,' admitted Ivory softly. But he had said she was beautiful, and he had behaved as though he very much wanted to see her again. But was an affair all he was after? It would be disappointing if it was, but no more than she could expect. She really ought to take her aunt's advice and forget him. The trouble was, she was half-way to being in love already!

She found it very difficult to concentrate on her work that day, and Mrs Trussell more than once had to pull her up for going into a daydream. When she arrived home Jacob was there and he must have convinced her aunt that his intentions were honourable because she looked as pleased to see him as she had the day before.

For the next two weeks she saw him regularly. He lavished her with presents, treating her as though she were a piece of Dresden china.

They visited theatres and restaurants, but very often sat in her aunt's front room which she had made available to them for his frequent visits. 'I am sure you want to be alone,' she had simpered, much to Ivory's amusement. Her change of face had been astounding.

It was rare Jacob talked about himself, except to say that when his father died his mother had remarried and gone to live in America. 'I used to spend as much time there as in England,' he said, 'but I'm too busy these days to pay them more than a flying visit. I've kept the family home going in Cornwall but I find London a much more convenient base to work from.'

Ivory was disappointed he never took her to his apartment, but could understand his reasons for not doing so. They were both so intensely emotionally involved that it would not be safe to be alone. She admired him for his self-discipline.

'I go to Cornwall to unwind,' he admitted. 'It's the only way these days that I get any peace and quiet. Even that was disrupted when I met you,' he added, his eyes twinkling kindly.

'Perhaps I should say I'm sorry, that I wish it had never happened?' she suggested impishly, cuddling up closer to him on her aunt's sofa.

He groaned and crushed her in his arms. 'Never, my Ivory. It was the best day of my life. You're very beautiful, and gracious, and utterly charming. You wear your clothes with the elegance of a woman who's had years and years of training—yet you're still young enough not to have lost your air of innocence. It's what I like about you best, my love. Please don't ever change.'

'I'll try not to,' she whispered shyly.

'When you get older you'll be absolutely stunning,' he added. 'I really am a most lucky man. It's my birthday in a few days' time, Ivory, I shall be thirty-five. Does that make me too old to ask you to marry me?'

Ivory's heart began a rapid, painful tattoo against her ribcage. 'You're joking! You don't mean that? I'm not your type. I don't live in your world.' It was what she wanted most of all, what she had hoped he would ask, but it frightened her half to death. Marriage to Jacob would mean mixing with his business associates, with a type of person she had never met before. She did not think she could handle it.

'Why do you think I've been chasing you?' he asked gently. 'I knew the instant I saw you that there could never be anyone else for me. My sweet, beautiful, Ivory, I want you to be my wife.'

She shook her head, her eyes blinded now with tears. 'No, Jacob, I can't. I'd fail you, I know that. I'm too young.'

'You mean I'm too old?' he suggested gruffly.

'No, never, it doesn't matter.'

She hated to see him tormented like this. She laid her hand on his face, feeling him tense at her touch.

'Then what, Ivory?' He pulled her hand to his mouth, covering it with urgent kisses. 'Don't you love me? Is there someone else? God, I can't bear the thought of you with another man.'

The pain on his face made Ivory cry out. 'You know there isn't. It's just that it's so sudden. I never expected it. Let me think about it, Jacob, please. It's too much to take in all at once.'

He shook his head and looked suddenly weary. 'What is there to think about? It should be a simple matter to say yes or no.'

She grimaced. 'I want to say yes, Jacob, believe me, I do. But it's not as easy as that. 'I'm not ready for marriage—my career—my shop—all that I've ever wanted—it . . .' They were excuses and she knew it.

'To hell with all that,' he cried savagely. 'When

you're married to me you won't have to work.
You'll have enough money to buy whatever you
want.' He pushed himself up and raked a hand
through his hair. 'I've made a mess of this,
haven't I, Ivory? I've asked you too soon. I
should have waited. But I'm not a patient man, as
you can see. I'll give you until tomorrow to make
up you mind. I'm going now. No—don't get up,
I'll see myself out.'

She felt strangely bereft when he had gone and
when her aunt came into the room she could have
screamed. 'Was that Jacob going?' asked Eleanor
mildly. 'Why didn't he say goodbye? Have you
quarrelled?' She looked intently at her niece's
anguished face. 'Why has he gone?'

Ivory was not usually rude to her aunt. They
enjoyed quite an excellent relationship considering the difference in their ages. But at this
moment she could not stand her aunt's natural
concern. 'It's none of your business,' she cried,
and rushed from the room.

Once she had calmed down she asked herself
why she had refused when it was what she
wanted most in the world. He excited her and she
wanted him to make love to her with a
desperation that sometimes frightened her. He
had proved he was after more than a simple
affair. He had treated her with respect and after
that first time he had never allowed his feelings to
get the better of him.

But shouldn't marriage be based on something
more than pure physical chemistry? Did she love
him enough to be able to cope with the sort of
lifestyle he would expect her to adopt? Once their
initial passion had burnt itself out would they still
have someting going for them? It was very easy to
get carried away, but she had heard enough about

marriages breaking up to know that it was not a commitment to be entered into lightly.

Jacob was so much more experienced than she. He knew exactly what he wanted out of life. She had thought she wanted her own business. How could she change her mind in two short weeks, when for the last twelve months she had thought of nothing else? If it was only infatuation she felt for Jacob it would be too late to do anything about it once they were married.

It was a relief to discover that her aunt had not risen when she went to work the next morning. She had spent a sleepless night pondering over her problem but was still no nearer to a solution.

It did not surprise her to discover that Jacob was at home once again when she got back, but it made her bite her lip nervously as she entered the room, wondering whether he had told her aunt of his proposal. Or whether he intended asking for her decision first before saying anything to Eleanor.

He rose immediately and walked towards her. He had never looked more devastating. His white shirt clung to his magnificently muscled chest, his black trousers revealed slim hips and long powerful legs, and his smile encompassed her completely. Hesitantly, suddenly shy, she allowed him to take her hands. She stood looking up at him, liking the comforting warmth that flowed through to her.

She searched his face for a clue as to how much he had said to her aunt. He smiled and his eyes crinkled at the corners and he looked kind and generous and she knew he would always look after her. He would cosset her, he would spoil her. She would be secure and very, very happy.

'I've told Eleanor,' he said softly. 'She's very happy for us and willingly gives her consent.'

'That I do,' said Eleanor immediately. 'You're a very lucky young girl, Ivory, and I wish your dear mother was alive to see what a good man you've chosen to marry.'

The matter was being taken out of her hands! Ivory looked in confusion from Jacob to her aunt, and then back to Jacob again. He smiled tenderly and bending his head kissed her lips. There was none of the passion that she usually associated with him. It was tender and reassuring, but nevertheless sent shivers shooting through her limbs and she trembled.

Although she had been sure that she would say yes, she experienced a moment's panic, and would have pulled away had he not anticipated her well. He slid his arms behind the small of her back and heedless that her aunt watched kissed her deeply and fiercely, going on and on until she felt dizzy from sheer lack of air. 'Don't let me down now, little one,' he mouthed hoarsely. 'I need you like I've never needed anyone in my whole life.'

The urgency in his tone convinced Ivory that he was speaking the truth. And if she was honest with herself she needed him too. She smiled weakly and nodded. 'I'll marry you, Jacob.' Her eyes were wide and beautiful, and moist with a gripping emotion that she felt would be with her for the rest of her life.

His reaction was staggering. He grinned and patted his pocket, a satisfied expression on his handsome face. 'I have a special licence here. We're getting married the day after tomorrow.'

Aunt Eleanor smiled also, evidently having been put in the picture already. 'I'm happy for you, Ivory. If I could have picked the man I would like you to marry I couldn't have chosen anyone more suited that Jacob. You make a handsome pair.'

She had changed, thought Ivory. Only two weeks ago she had told her that he was not her type, that he was far too rich and successful, that he had a reputation that was not quite nice. Oh, how she had changed.

The next morning he came round early and took her to the shop where she worked. He had a quiet word with Mrs Trussell, who wished Ivory every future happiness and looked at her with new respect. Jacob Pendragon had made a definite impression.

Then he took her shopping for her trousseau, and bought the biggest diamond engagement ring she had ever seen. She was awed by its magnificence and it felt strange and heavy on her finger. Afterwards it was lunch and a steady ride home. He left her at the door, refusing her invitation to come in. 'Get your packing done and have an early night,' he ordered, not unkindly. 'You have a big day tomorrow. I'm afraid we'll have to delay the honeymoon.' He kissed her tenderly. 'You don't mind?'

'So long as I'm with you,' she said, and wondered why she felt close to tears.

Sensing her emotion Jacob pulled her roughly against him. 'We're going to be happy, I promise you that. You have nothing at all to fear, my beautiful little Ivory.'

Ivory wished she could be as sure. It was all happening so swiftly she did not have time to think. Most girls planned their wedding months and months beforehand with stars in their eyes and dreams in their head. She was missing out on all that. She was being pushed into something she was not quite sure she was ready for.

It was a very quiet wedding with only her aunt, Debby and Clair, who had been amazed and delighted to hear the news, and a couple of Jacob's friends who were also his business colleagues attending.

David and Martin went a little above Ivory's head but nevertheless she managed to hold her own, cocooned in the knowledge that at least Jacob loved her, that she meant more to him than any other woman he had met.

It was a satisfying feeling and she sailed through the ceremony with her head held high, a sparkle in her lovely brown eyes, and a flush of happiness to her cheeks.

The heavy gold band Jacob placed on her finger matched the exquisite engagement ring, and his kiss to seal their alliance held a promise of things to come.

After the short reception at her aunt's home they left for Jacob's apartment. Although the drive would take little more than half an hour she felt as if they were going to the other side of the world, and there was a dryness to her mouth and an uncontrolled beating to her heart.

It occurred to her that she was married to a man whom she knew little or nothing about. She was Mrs Jacob Pendragon and later he would expect her to share his bed. The very thought sent cold shivers down her spine. Would he be gentle? Would he take into account the fact that she was a virgin? Or would he be like a wild animal now that she was legally his? She had had a taste of the passion that raged inside him.

It made her realise how inexperienced she was. Panic welled and she played nervously with the rings on her finger. Before she could stop herself she cried out.

Jacob turned and smiling gently took her hand.
'Feeling jittery? There's no need. I won't harm
you, Ivory. You're very precious to me, and I
shall treat you accordingly.'

'It's happened so quickly,' she whispered. 'I'm
scared. I'm not sure that I'm capable of being the
sort of wife you want.'

'Would I have chosen you otherwise?' There
was a confident curve to his lips as he kept his
eyes on the road ahead. 'Why do you think I've
waited all these years before getting married?
You're the one I've been waiting for, my little
innocent, and my pleasure will be in teaching
you, helping you become a loving and caring
woman.'

His apartment was much bigger than she
expected. She had imagined him to have a
bachelor flat with just the basic necessities, but
instead his penthouse suite was bigger even than
her aunt's house. Ivory wandered from room to
room, conscious that she was doing this merely to
escape Jacob, but also marvelling at his exquisite
taste in furniture and design.

The huge window in the lounge had a
panoramic view over the city and she stood for a
few minutes picking out the various landmarks.
The floor was thickly carpeted and she did not
hear Jacob come up behind her. When he slid his
arms about her waist she gave a squeak of
surprise, but when he gently turned her and held
her slim shaking body close it was as though the
warmth and strength of him flowed into her.
Within seconds she began to relax, lifting her
face, accepting his infinitely tender kiss.

Jacob did not press his attentions on her. He
was attuned to her every thought, aware of each
spasm of emotion, conscious of her need to be

treated with utmost gentleness. He had been patient for this long, she thought, he could afford to be patient for a little while longer—and she loved him all the more for it.

She drew in a quick breath and pressed herself closer to him. 'I think I'm ready for you now, Jacob,' she husked, and felt his shuddering response.

He cupped her face with his warm brown hands and looked at her for several long heart-stopping minutes, his eyes glittering with hunger and desire, his breathing as rapid and shallow as her own.

Then with a groan he caught her to him, his mouth fastening on hers in a kiss that was as devastating as it was bruising. He plundered the sweet softness of her mouth, shaking in his passion, more worked-up than she had ever seen him before.

He swung her up into his arms and carried her through to the bedroom, laying her down on the big soft bed. Expertly and with tantalising slowness he took off the cream silk dress she had worn for her wedding, the lacy underwear he had chosen himself, until she lay naked and vulnerable, her wide eyes almost filling her face.

She felt embarrassingly shy, but knew that Jacob would not like it if she attempted to cover herself up, and made herself submit to the thorough examination he gave her as he dragged off his own clothes.

'You're very lovely.' He, too, was full of emotion.

'You're quite something yourself,' she husked, feasting her eyes on his magnificent chest and the rock-hard flatness of his stomach. That day at the pool they had seen each other in only the briefest of garments, but this was something different. She felt that not only were they stripped of their clothes, but their defences as well.

He was potent, like a heady wine, and she felt her senses spinning as he lowered himself on the bed beside her. They came together as though this was what they had been waiting for all their lives.

His long hard fingers stroked and tormented every inch of her body, tracing every curve, and she felt as though she was being driven out of her mind.

She writhed and arched herself towards him, feeling the heat of his desire, running her fingertips over the hard silken smoothness of his back. He thrust a leg between her thighs and a host of new and challenging emotions were aroused in her.

Her breasts ached with an agony of longing and when his hot mouth slid down the thrusting column of her throat to move with tantalising slowness over the burgeoning fullness of her breasts, finally closing his lips over one hard nipple, she felt a white hot explosion inside her stomach.

She cried out and threaded her fingers through his hair, holding him close one minute and pulling his hair in an agony of longing the next. 'Make love to me, Jacob,' she cried in anguish. 'Please love me.'

When their bodies finally merged she felt a soaring excitement that she had never imagined possible, and only the briefest stab of pain. Wild sensations robbed her of all coherent thought and she wanted his lovemaking to go on and on for ever.

Jacob seemed to lose control, and she guessed

that he had waited for this moment so long it was as intoxicating for him as it was for her. They were so completely in accord that the fierceness of their actions drove them to a pinnacle of supreme ecstasy and ultimate satisfaction.

Afterwards he pulled her into his arms, drawing her comfortingly against his overheated body. 'That, my beautiful Ivory, was quite something. Don't ever let me hear you say again that you can't be the sort of wife I want. No one else could ever satisfy me in that same way.'

She felt humble, as all she had done was allow her own body to respond in whatever way it wanted. But if that was what Jacob needed, then she was prepared to give herself to him at any time of the night or day.

CHAPTER THREE

CURLED up beside Jacob, his arm protectively about her, Ivory slept, a contented smile curving her lips. When she awoke she was alone, a slender package in the place Jacob had lain.

He came into the room as she began to open it. He was fresh from the shower and completely naked. Ivory rested her eyes for a moment on the magnificence of his body and decided she would never get over having such an exciting man for a husband.

Fresh quivers of emotion raged through her as he tenderly smiled down. 'Open your parcel,' he said. 'A gift to the most beautiful bride in the world.'

Ivory looked at him with wide sad eyes. 'Oh, Jacob, I haven't bought you a present. I never thought. I don't seem to have had much time to think of anything.'

He cupped her chin with warm firm fingers and looked deep into her eyes. 'You've given yourself to me, my love. That is all I ever want.' His hand trailed down her throat to the flickering pulse at its base, lingering on the perfect smoothness of her breasts. He groaned and moved away. 'Hell, Ivory, I want you again. Open that damn parcel, for pity's sake. I need something to take my mind off you.'

Too shy to admit that she wanted him too, Ivory slid off the pink satiny paper with its pattern of hearts and wedding bells, and with fingers that shook uncontrollably opened the ivory leather case she found inside.

'Jacob, you shouldn't!' Tears welled as she looked down at the gold necklace with its one perfect diamond dropper in the centre, and a pair of exquisite earrings to match. They must have cost a small fortune—and he had already spent so much on her!

'How can I thank you?' she husked. 'You really shouldn't buy me all these presents. I don't deserve them.'

'In my eyes you do,' he said thickly, lifting the necklace from its satin bed and fastening it around Ivory's neck, then fixing the earrings in place and sitting back on his heels to study the effect.

'If I had my way,' he grinned, 'you'd never wear anything else. There's something erotic about gold jewellery and naked skin. I think I'm going to have to make love to you again.'

Before the end of the day Ivory had lost her shyness. She knew Jacob's body as intimately as she knew her own. It amazed her how completely in accord they were. Her need of him was equal to his need of her. She had never realised that making love could be so beautiful and satisfying.

She woke the following morning to find the bed empty beside her. In place of Jacob's dark head was a slip of paper. She felt crushingly disappointed when she discovered he had gone to the office to keep a prior appointment.

He had not wanted to spoil her day yesterday, he said, by telling her, but hoped she would understand. He had put some money in her handbag and suggested she went shopping. He would be back in time for dinner.

She felt choked and as frustrated as a child who has been told a special treat is suddenly off. 'Damn you, Jacob,' she said strongly. 'You can't do this to me.' But he had! She ought to have realised when he said they would have to delay their honeymoon. But she had expected more than one day! Never had she imagined that he would go back to work straight away.

He had made her give up her job. What was she to do now? How on earth was she going to fill her time? Go shopping, he had said. Heavens, he had already bought her enough clothes to last a lifetime. She liked beautiful clothes and enjoyed wearing them, but was never extravagant. She could never afford to be.

But she could now! Right, Jacob, she said to herself. You suggested it, so don't blame me if I go overboard. In actual fact she thoroughly enjoyed herself. She shopped at Harrods and Jaeger and all the places she could never afford to go to before. She bought Jacob a Shetland sweater for his birthday the next day, hoping he would like it, unsure what to buy a man who has everything.

When she got home she had a wonderful time trying on her new clothes and it was not until late afternoon that she gave any thought to their evening meal. Jacob would expect his dinner ready. Indeed, perhaps that was what some of the money had been for!

She went hot at the thought that there might not be any food in the kitchen. Not that she was a very good cook. Her aunt had not allowed her to help often as she was a very fastidious and tidy person and could not bear the thought of anyone making a mess in her kitchen.

When she heard a key in the lock and she still had her purchases spread about the room, she felt suddenly uncomfortable. He would think she was behaving like a spoilt child instead of a responsible married woman.

But it was not Jacob who entered, instead a plump motherly woman with a bag full of groceries and a cheerful smile on her face. She took in the untidy lounge at a glance but did not bat an eyelid. 'Mrs Pendragon?' she enquired expectantly.

Ivory nodded. It was the first time anyone had called her by this name. She rather liked it. 'Who are you?'

'Humphrey,' said the woman. 'Mrs Humphrey to be exact, but Jacob always calls me Humphrey. I'm his daily, didn't he tell you? I also prepare his meals when he's at home or entertaining. May I offer you my congratulations? You've been shopping, I see. Lucky you, marrying someone like Jacob. Now me, I have to watch every penny I spend. Mind you, Jacob's more than generous. I can't complain. I'm late today. My sister's ill. I expect you thought I wasn't coming?'

Ivory's head began to whirl. The woman sounded as though she was prepared to go on for ever. She shook her head and smiled. 'Actually Jacob didn't tell me about you. I was just wondering what to do for dinner.'

'Just like a man,' declared Humphrey. 'Never mind, I'm here now, dearie. Shall I put these things away for you? My, aren't they lovely? Are you a model? You certainly look like one. I wish I was as slim as you, but I like my food too much. I have some cream cakes in my bag, would you like one with a nice cup of tea? I could certainly do with a rest. I've been on my feet all day.'

'I'll put them away myself,' laughed Ivory, 'and no thanks, I don't want a cake, but a cup of tea would certainly be welcome.'

Jacob had put his own clothes into one of the

other bedrooms, leaving Ivory with a wide
expanse of mirrored wardrobe that entirely filled
one wall.

She had laughed and said she could never
possibly use all that space, but looking at her
possessions now she was not so sure that he had
been wrong. What did seem wrong was for one
person to own so much. She must have been out
of her mind.

The daily called her when the tea was ready
and afterwards Ivory spent her time soaking in
the deep sunken bath in their en-suite bathroom.
It was out of this world with its gold-plated
fittings. At the touch of a button powerful jets of
water whirled about her body, refreshing and
invigorating, making her feel like a new woman.
Ivory decided she could get used to this life
without any difficulty at all.

It took her a long time to decide what to wear.
Eventually, assuming they would stay in for the
evening, she selected a flowing kaftan in pink shot
silk, belting it tightly about her slim waist, and
slipping her feet into high-heeled satin mules. She
brushed her hair until it shone and left it loose
about her shoulders the way Jacob liked it.

Mrs Humphrey left shortly after six, confirm-
ing that their dinner was all ready and was being
kept warm in the heated food trolley. 'You're as
radiant as any bride I've seen,' were her parting
words. 'If I know Jacob he'll be home early
tonight.'

But he wasn't. The telephone rang at seven,
just as Ivory was beginning to go out of her mind
with worry. 'Jacob, is that you?' she enquired
breathlessly.

'Ivory.' The deep sensual growl affected her
just as deeply over the 'phone as it did when he

was near. 'I'm awfully sorry, my love, I can't get away. It will be another hour at least. You'd better eat without me.'

Ivory swallowed her disappointment. 'It's all right, Jacob, I'll wait.' How often, she wondered, did this happen? He had not prepared her for this. She had no idea. He had spent so much time with her this last couple of weeks she imagined that he did not do very much at all.

'I've missed you,' he said thickly. 'Hell, I'd give anything to get out of this. Just be ready when I come home, will you?'

'I'm ready now,' she whispered huskily, her pulses beginning to race.

He groaned and she closed her eyes as shivers of anticipation ran through her limbs. 'Oh, Ivory! You don't know what you do to me.'

If it was the same as he was doing to her then she did know. 'I'll see you later,' she breathed and put the phone down before things began to get out of hand. She would never have believed that she could feel so excited simply by hearing his voice. He, too, had been affected and it gave her a wonderful heady feeling of power to be able to do this to him.

She curled on a fur-covered sofa and wrapped her arms about herself, hugging close the memories of last night's lovemaking, looking forward to a repeat of the same performance.

But an hour passed, and then two, and it was after ten before she finally heard his key in the lock. Her warm feelings had changed to anger and she greeted him coolly as he came into the room.

He looked tired but she ignored that, demanding in a high tight voice, 'So you have finally decided to come? I was just going to bed, I'm very tired. Good night, Jacob.'

She turned her back and began to walk towards their bedroom, but she had taken no more than a couple of steps before he was behind her, spinning her round to face him, holding her in a grip that held no mercy.

'Oh, no you don't. I've had a hell of a day, Ivory, and I need you like I've never needed you before.' His face was creased in a torment of desire and anger, his blue eyes hungrily devouring her. His mouth fixed on hers before she could say another word and she knew that her token gesture had been in vain.

Once he had taken his fill of her mouth he threw off his jacket and released his tie, opening his shirt. He raked his hands through his hair and sat down on the sofa, holding out his arms for Ivory to join him.

Willingly now she sat on his lap, linking her hands behind his neck, pulling his head towards hers. When he slid his hand inside her kaftan and discovered that she was wearing nothing at all underneath he tensed and groaned yet again. 'You've been waiting for me—like this?'

She nodded, love shining in her eyes.

'Oh, God, and I've been sitting in a stuffy room discussing new marketing techniques.'

'That's your fault,' she said primly. 'You should have told them that you now have a wife—a very demanding wife—who objects to every minute you spend away from her.'

She had no hesitation now in initiating their lovemaking, and she finished unbuttoning his shirt, tugging it free before pressing passionate kisses to his sensual hair-roughened skin.

It must have been midnight before either of them thought about food. By then the meal Mrs Humphrey had left was unpalatable and they settled for huge chunks of cheese and apple, washed down with a bottle of white wine.

As Ivory had eaten nothing all day she felt distinctly light-headed by the time they went to bed and passed out straight away, not waking until Mrs Humphrey raised the blinds at the windows.

'It's almost noon,' announced the woman. 'Jacob left a note that I was to wake you if you weren't already up. He wants you to look extra special this evening. He's left you some money in case you need to buy a new dress.

Ivory laughed. 'He hasn't seen what I bought yesterday!' But it was typical of him. He was so generous it was ridiculous. But guests for dinner! On his birthday too! She wasn't so sure she would be able to cope. She had never, ever, in her whole life, done any entertaining, nor had her aunt. Eleanor was the sort of person who kept herself very much to herself.

'I'm not expected to cook the meal, am I?' she exclaimed in horror, sitting up suddenly, forgetting she was stark naked. When she realised she pulled the sheet up to her chin and could not quite meet Mrs Humphrey's eye.

'Don't be embarrassed in front of me, lovey,' laughed the woman. 'I have teenage daughters of my own and they're always parading about in next to nothing. As for dinner, all you'll have to do is serve it up. I'll do the necessary.'

'Thank goodness,' breathed Ivory. Nevertheless she was still daunted by the prospect of playing hostess to Jacob's friends.

She got up and took a quick shower, then pulled on a blue jumpsuit that was one of her latest purchases, tying her hair back with a ribbon so that she looked about fifteen once again.

Afterwards she joined the daily in the kitchen for cold chicken and salad, followed by a delicious apple pie that had been baked for them the night before. Then the woman shooed her out while she got on with her preparations for the evening ahead.

Ivory spent at least an hour trying on one dress after another, finally deciding on a tight black dress with a deep vee at the back and long ruched sleeves. A wide belt emphasised her narrow waist and she looked more elegant than she felt. It was only at a time like this that it bothered her how much older Jacob was.

She was ready two hours before she need have been, pacing nervously up and down the room Mrs Humphrey left after she had set the table and reassured Ivory that all she had to do was bring the dishes to it.

But Ivory was not reassured and before she finally heard Jacob and his guests talking outside the door she had drunk a couple of glasses of whisky.

She felt a little better when she discovered that two of their visitors were women. Jacob introduced her with pride to Rose, a brittle blonde who was David's wife, and Julie, a sultry brunette, married to Martin. The two men she already knew, of course, having met them only two days earlier at her wedding.

They were all in their late thirties, sophisticated, self-assured, and treated her with amused tolerance. 'Jacob's child bride,' Rose called her, much to Ivory's annoyance, and she had a feeling that the evening was going to be a disaster before it began.

Nevertheless, for Jacob's sake, she was determined not to let these people put her down, and she drank and laughed and talked as much as the rest of them, showing a keen interest when they discussed business, and revealing that she knew quite as much about world affairs as any of them.

She began to feel that after all she had been worrying for nothing when Rose suddenly said, 'I don't know what Valma's going to say when she discovers you're married, Jacob. She'll hit the roof. She's always considered you her private property.'

Jacob looked unconcerned. 'That's her bad luck, Rose. There was never anything serious between us.'

'That wasn't what she liked to think,' pressed the blonde, giving Ivory a sly look.

Ivory did her best not to let this woman's catty remarks hurt, but there was no denying that she felt as though someone had suddenly slit her throat. She went very quiet and reached out for her drink to steady her leaping nerves. Unfortunately she looked across at Jacob as she did so and caught the bottle instead with her outstretched hand. The red wine they were drinking with their Beef Chasseur spilled across the table and on to the front of Rose's white silk dress.

'You clumsy little fool!' she cried savagely. 'You did that deliberately.'

Ivory went hot and tried to apologise, but Rose would not listen. 'You've ruined my dress,' she shrieked. 'Just look at it!'

'I'll fetch a cloth,' said Ivory, pushing back her chair, catching the heel of her shoe against the leg in her haste and tripping so that she stumbled against Rose's husband.

'My God!' exclaimed the woman. 'What have you married, Jacob—a schoolgirl? Doesn't she know how to behave?'

Jacob's lips were grim as he came to Ivory's aid, putting his arm comfortingly across her shaking shoulders. 'Accidents happen, Rose,' he said quietly. 'It's unfortunate, but it's one of those things. Ivory, take Rose to our room. She can change into something of yours. I'll see that your dress is cleaned and returned, Rose.'

'No thank you,' said Rose shrilly. 'I want to go home. David—please, my coat.'

But Jacob insisted that she stay, much to Ivory's chargrin. She would have preferred them all to leave. She wanted to be alone with her humiliation. She had let Jacob down and was thoroughly ashamed.

In their bedroom she opened her wardrobe and planned on leaving Rose to it, but the older woman called her back. 'Was it me mentioning our dear friend, Valma, that made you suddenly jittery?' she asked, her eyes glittering.

Ivory tossed her head and tried to pretend a nonchalance that she was far from feeling. 'Of course not. Like Jacob said it was an accident. It could have happened to anyone.'

'Especially if they'd just found out about their husband's former lover?' The red lips curved into a sneer. 'I should imagine it would be a bit much for someone as young and trusting as you to swallow. I've watched your big brown eyes on Jacob tonight. You should learn not to wear your heart on your sleeve, my dear. Jacob's not the perfect husband you seem to think.'

Quite how she stopped herself from flying across the room and scratching the other woman's face Ivory did not know. 'What Jacob did before he married me is no business of mine,' she said tightly.

'How about last night?' Rose's tones were

honeyed. 'I must admit when Dave told me that Jacob was joining them at the club I was a teeny bit surprised, considering he had only got married the day before. But now I've met you, well, I suppose it's understandable. Jacob needs a woman, my dear, not a gauche little schoolgirl. Not that he'd ever admit he'd made a mistake. Valma would have made him a perfect wife. She thought so, too, in case you didn't know. I'd like to see her face when she comes back and finds him married. She'll be absolutely livid. I must say, I wouldn't like to be in your shoes.'

Ivory could not take it any longer. She shrieked and lunged at Rose, catching hold of her hair and pulling mercilessly. 'You bitch!' she cried, tears racing down her cheeks.

'Get away from me!' Rose pushed her forcefully and Ivory stumbled across the room. At that moment the door opened and Jacob came in. He looked from one to the other, his murderous expression reminding Ivory of that first day they had met.

'What on earth is going on? Ivory? Rose?'

Ivory picked herself up but said nothing, looking down at the floor, realising how badly she had behaved.

'We had a disagreement,' said Rose. 'I think you've made a mistake in marrying that one, Jacob. She's really nothing better than a gutter-snipe.'

'When I want you opinion I'll ask for it,' he rasped coldly, and Ivory felt a small measure of satisfaction. 'I think it might be best if you left after all, Rose. Martin and Julie are going too. I apologise if the evening has not been the success I had hoped.'

Ivory did not move until they had both gone

from the room, then she sat on the edge of the bed and hugged her arms around her, shivering with cold and shame and wondering how she would ever be able to make it up to him.

At least he was not blaming her, that was something. He had seemed more annoyed with Rose—and the woman deserved it. She had been hateful. She wondered who this Valma person was, but decided that Rose had been exaggerating. She seemed the type who would derive much pleasure from playing one woman against another. Whatever Valma had once been to Jacob it made no difference now. It was herself he had chosen to marry.

At last their guests went and she looked up, smiling tremulously, as Jacob came into the room. 'Oh, Jacob,' she began. 'I'm so sorry. What must you be thinking?'

She was entirely unprepared for his anger and cringed away when he bore down on her with a fearsome expression on his face. 'How dare you assault one of my friends,' he yelled. 'I was relying on you to make a good impression.'

'If people like Rose are your friends, then I don't think I care much for them,' she returned heatedly. 'Doesn't it matter that she was insulting me?'

'I don't believe that,' he said, nostrils flaring wide, blue eyes as cold as chips of ice. 'She was a little upset because you had ruined her dress, but—'

'You didn't hear what she said to me in here,' flung Ivory.

The thick brows rose. 'Perhaps you'd care to enlighten me?'

'I'd rather not,' she said miserably, knowing that in the mood he was in he would not believe her.

'Suit yourself.' He took off his jacket and tie and flung them down on a chair. 'You do realise I'll be a laughing stock at the office tomorrow?'

'I'm sure your shoulders are broad enough to take it,' she cried, incited to further anger. 'I should imagine my behaviour tonight merely confirmed the opinion your colleagues already have of me.'

'And what is that supposed to mean?' he rasped coldly, pausing in the act of ripping open his shirt, treating her to a piercing glance from those icy blue eyes.

Ivory held his gaze as best she could. 'No man who is completely satisfied with his new bride would join his business friends at the club the day after he was married.'

'If that is what Rose told you than I blame you for believing her.' His tough square chin jutted mercilessly. 'That woman thrives on scandal— true or not. I should have warned you.'

'If you'd had any thought at all for me you wouldn't have brought her here,' cried Ivory. 'I'm not used to being married yet. I could certainly do without being thrown in at the deep end. And why would she say you were at your club if you weren't?'

'We were,' he admitted surprisingly. 'We finished our discussions over a drink. It's a thing we often do. The atmosphere is more congenial. We seem to get through more that way.'

Ivory began to feel deflated. 'Why didn't you tell me then? Rose made it sound as though you had no desire to come home at all.'

He shrugged and finished taking off his shirt. 'It's a normal thing with us. I never gave it a thought.' He pulled off his trousers and they joined the heap, then he disappeared into the bathroom and she heard him splashing under the shower before brushing his teeth.

When he returned she was still sitting on the edge of the bed. 'Come on to bed,' he said, not unkindly.

Ivory looked at him with wide sad eyes. 'Who's Valma? Why haven't you told me about her?'

'Hell!' he snarled. 'If we're going to have an inquisition on all the girls I've ever dated in the past we'll be here all night. She's no one you need concern your pretty head about.'

'Rose seemed to think she was.' Ivory pushed herself up and began struggling with the zip at the back of her dress. 'She said she'll be mad when she discovers you've married me.'

'That's her bad luck,' said Jacob rudely. 'I never promised her anything.'

'But you were—lovers?' She swallowed painfully, wondering why she was torturing herself like this.

He shook his head impatiently. 'I've never claimed to have led a saint's life, for pity's sake. Hell, what is this? I've married you, doesn't that tell you anything? I don't want any other woman now. I want you.'

That should have pleased her but somehow she felt sadder still. She tugged angrily at the zip and it stuck fast. Tears sprang to her eyes and she stamped her foot.

'Here, let me.' Jacob's voice was infinitely gentle now, his fingers warm against her skin. In a couple of seconds he had released the offending zip and slid the dress from her shoulders. Then he turned her round and held her close, his arms binding her, his heart thudding against her shoulder.

Gradually Ivory's tension eased and when she

finally gave a shuddering sigh and turned her face
to him he scooped her into his arms and lowered
her to the bed. His passionate lovemaking made
her forget her doubts and when she finally went
to sleep Ivory was as sure of his love as she had
been before Rose had sown the seeds of poison.

The next morning Jacob was still beside her
when she awoke. He was studying her with that
hungry look in his eyes that she was beginning to
recognise. She smiled blissfully. 'Aren't you
going to work today?'

'Later,' he gruffed. 'I have some private
business to attend to first.' His mouth closed on
hers before she could say another word and there
was something incredibly beautiful about being
made love to before she had had time to wake up
properly.

She felt very close to Jacob at times like this
and it was easy to forget that all too soon she
would be on her own again. She wanted him to
stay here for ever. She wanted to spend the rest
of her life in bed making love.

When he finally tore himself away he said,
'Ivory, I want to apologise for last night. It was
far too soon for me to spring anything like that on
you. I should have known you aren't yet up to
that sort of thing.'

She slid her fingers over the firm smoothness
of his back. 'I did try. If it hadn't been for Rose
and her sly digs I think I'd have coped. She made
me nervous. I've never had to entertain before. I
expect I'll get used to it.' Although she hoped she
would never get silly and brittle like his
colleagues' wives. Their incessant chatter about
nothing in particular had jarred her nerves.

'I reckon Rose got what she deserved with that
wine,' he grinned surprisingly, 'but sometimes,

Ivory, I entertain important customers. If you did the same to them it could mean losing valuable business.'

She pulled a wry face. 'Why didn't you tell me it was a hostess you were after, not a wife?'

'Because it wouldn't be true, my love, and you know it.' He caught her to him and kissed her savagely. 'Mmm, you make me feel good. I think I might just spend the day at home.'

'You will?' There was an eagerness on Ivory's face that made him groan.

'Oh, that I could. But you see, my sweet, I've already neglected my work because of you. Now I must catch up—and the quicker I do it the sooner we will have our honeymoon. I can't wait for that. I promise you then that I'll devote every second of my time to you. You'll be so fed up of me that you'll beg me to go out.'

'Never!' Ivory laughingly shook her head. 'I love you so much, Jacob, it's unbelievable. Thank you, *thank you*, for marrying me.'

'Hell, don't thank me,' he protested gruffly. 'It's my pleasure as much as yours. I've never met a woman who satisfies me as completely as you. You're pretty fantastic, do you know that?'

'I'm glad,' she said shyly. 'I thought I might be too young and inexperienced.'

'That's part of your charm. You're so natural. I really think I must be the luckiest man in the whole world.' He heaved a sigh and dragged himself off the bed. 'And now, much as I hate the idea, I must get ready.'

'I'll cook your breakfast,' offered Ivory immediately.

But he shook his head. 'A glass of orange is all I ever have in the mornings—and lashings of coffee when I get to the office. Stay there, my love. You've a life of leisure now, don't forget. Enjoy it while you can. Once we start a family there'll be no more lie-ins.'

Ivory had not thought about babies yet, but she realised now that it was a very strong possibility. She might even be pregnant already! The thought made her smile happily. 'How many children do you want, Jacob? I think four would be nice, two boys and two girls. I always used to wish I had some brothers and sisters.'

'If it's four you want then four it will be,' he laughed. 'But I'm afraid I can't guarantee the sex.'

It was not until he was showering that Ivory remembered she had not yet given him his birthday present. Yesterday had been such a total disaster that she had forgotten all about it. She placed the package on the bed and waited shyly and anxiously for his reaction.

His brows shot up questioningly when he saw it.

'Your birthday present,' she explained softly. 'I'm sorry it's a day late.'

He groaned. 'I'd forgotten all about it myself. How could I? My love, I'm so sorry. I would never have brought my visitors back if I'd remembered. It completely slipped my mind. What a fiasco it was as well. It's certainly a birthday I shall never forget.' He opened his parcel and exclaimed over the patterned sweater.

'It's quite the most beautiful present I've ever had. Thank you, my darling.' He took her into his arms and Ivory felt a glow of warmth and comfort as his mouth found hers.

When he eventually left she took a shower and put on a pair of tight white jeans and a shocking pink top that stopped just short of her waist.

She felt happy and carefree as she picked up the clothes Jacob had discarded the night before and took them through into the next bedroom. It was the first time she had looked inside his wardrobe and she was amazed at the number of suits and jackets that he possessed. Shirts, too, all on individual hangers. It was a good job he had moved them out to make room for hers. They would never have fitted them all in.

Not until she was closing the door did she spot the black frill. Pulling back Jacob's raincoat she discovered a sheer nightdress and matching négligé, as well as a couple of evening dresses.

Her heart stopped beating as she gazed at the offending garments. No wonder he had emptied his wardrobe! But at least he could have hidden them a little better.

She knew without question to whom they belonged and felt agonisingly jealous all of a sudden, even though she knew she ought not to. Valma was a part of his past, he had told her that, and she had no reason to disbelieve him.

But Valma was away. On holiday presumably. What would happen when she returned? A cold hand clutched at her heart before she told herself that she was being stupid. Jacob had chosen to marry her, not Valma. There was nothing at all for her to worry about.

She closed the door hurriedly and because she needed to keep herself occupied began to clear up the remains of last night's meal. Jacob had told her to leave it for Humphrey, but she could not sit down and do nothing. But even though her hands were busy it did not stop her mind from working, and the more she thought about this unknown woman the more jealous she became.

In the end she could remain in the flat no

longer. She snatched up her handbag and let herself out, bumping into Mrs Humphrey at the door. The woman was talking to a man but upon seeing Ivory she said, 'Ah, here is Mrs Pendragon now. Ivory, guess what your loving husband has bought you now?'

Ivory had no idea, nor did she want to know. All she wanted to do was get away. But she knew it would be unforgivable to ignore the excited woman so she gave a little sigh and said impatiently, 'You tell me.'

Mrs Humphrey dangled a set of keys in front of Ivory's face. 'A new car. Isn't that fantastic?'

Ivory looked from her to the man who was nodding his agreement. She felt in a daze and it was difficult to make herself smile. She was not so sure that she wanted to accept, not so sure that she liked Jacob buying her all these expensive presents.

Then she realised how much more freedom it would give her. She would be able to go and see her aunt whenever she liked without waiting for Jacob, or catching a bus or a train. She would no longer be tied to the flat when Jacob was at work. It opened up a whole new horizon.

She took the keys from Mrs Humphrey. 'Where is it? I'll go for a spin now.'

The delivery man showed her where it was parked and at first Ivory was too dazed to do anything other than stand and stare. She had expected a Mini, or something equally as nondescript. Instead it was a silver sports car with a long bonnet and headlights that flipped up when you put them on.

She wondered whether she would be able to handle it, but after the man had shown her the controls and she had driven it a couple of times round the car park that belonged to the block of flats, she felt quite at home.

Immediately she decided to visit her aunt and when she drew up outside a half hour later Eleanor could not believe her eyes. 'It shows how much Jacob loves you,' she said with satisfaction. 'You've really done well for yourself, Ivory. I'm so pleased.'

Eleanor cooked an omelette for their lunch and wanted to know everything that had happened since she had left home. Ivory told her about the disaster with the bottle of wine, leaving out Rose's snide remarks, making a joke out of the whole thing.

Her aunt looked horrified at first, then said strongly, 'He shouldn't have expected so much of you. But perhaps it's my fault, I've never really trained you for that sort of thing. I didn't think you'd marry such a well-heeled gentleman.'

'Don't worry about it,' smiled Ivory, 'I'm not.'

She wished she could confide in her aunt about Valma, how she felt that she posed a threat to their marriage. But Eleanor would not understand. She was a firm believer that there was one man for one woman in this world, and did not believe in divorce. If Ivory hinted that there could be another woman in Jacob's life at this stage in their marriage she would be appalled.

When she got back home Jacob was there and he was so loving and attentive that she decided she was worrying for nothing.

Over the next few days all thoughts of the unknown Valma faded from her mind and at last came the day when Jacob announced he could now take two weeks off from his work for their postponed honeymoon.

'Where are we going?' she asked eagerly.

He smiled tenderly. 'I'm going to be very selfish and very possessive. I want to share you with no one. We're going home, to Cornwall, to the house where I spent my childhood. No one will disturb us there. I hope you'll learn to love it as much as I do.'

She pretended to be disappointed. 'I thought it would be the Bahamas at least. Have you no exotic villas abroad?'

He shook his head ruefully. 'I'm afraid not. My tastes are simple.'

'You disappoint me,' she cried. 'I was looking forward to getting a tropical tan.'

'You wouldn't get that anyway,' he grinned. 'I intend spending the whole two weeks in bed.'

Ivory shivered deliciously. 'Why didn't you warn me I was marrying a sex maniac?'

'Are you complaining?' he asked sternly.

For an answer she snuggled up against him and it was not long before they were lost once again in the heat of their passion.

On their drive down to Cornwall Ivory questioned Jacob about his house. 'It's on Bodmin Moor,' he explained. 'It's big and old and some say it's gloomy. It's called Blackstone. It's the perfect escape when you want to get away from it all.'

'I thought, when I met you,' she said, 'that you lived in Cornwall permanently. You seemed to belong.'

'I like to think I do,' he smiled. 'I spend as much time there as work permits.'

It was early evening when they reached the moor. They turned off the main road just a little way past Jamaica Inn, making Ivory realise how close they had been to his home that day. The lane got narrower and narrower until finally it was nothing more than a rough dirt track, and all around them stretched a vast sweeping landscape dotted with stunted bushes, and trees bowed by the harsh winter winds.

Occasionally she glimpsed water, a narrow stream chasing its way across country, and there was miles and miles of green springy turf and yellow gorse. Birds circled above and hunted for food. It was incredibly peaceful, as he had said, but also, she guessed, it could be painfully lonely.

Without warning they were upon the house, big and daunting, built of slate and granite and blackened with age. It had a neglected air about it, which was surprising considering Jacob's wealth, and Ivory felt her spirits drop. She was to spend her honeymoon here? In this ugly house that looked cold and dead, where no windows sparkled in the sun.

'Is this it?' she asked incredulously.

He smiled and nodded. 'This is it, my sweet. I'm afraid the old place doesn't get the attention it should. I look after it myself.'

He stopped the car on what once must have been a cobbled drive, but which now was overgrown with grass and weeds. They climbed out and Ivory flexed her arms and legs which had grown stiff after the long drive, and tried not to look too disappointed.

Jacob unlocked the front door with its coat of peeling paint, swung it wide, then without a word lifted her into his arms and carried her across the threshold.

'Welcome to Blackstone,' he said proudly.

Ivory repressed a shudder and allowed him to kiss her. Soon, as was always the way, his warmth and strength flowed into her and she began to relax. She even managed to laugh at her own misgivings.

He showed her the house. The kitchen that looked as though it belonged to another era. The dining room and living room with their ancient furniture. Various other rooms that were not in use, where the furniture was shrouded with sheets making them look ghostly and eerie so that she clung to his hand and quickly edged her way out.

Upstairs the bathroom had a big old-fashioned bath that was stained brown in places. Nothing at all like the smart shining one in his flat. She wondered if the plumbing worked.

There were countless bedrooms, each as dark and dismal as the next. The one that was to be theirs housed a huge double bed with a throwover tapestry quilt in dark chocolate brown. The furniture was dark too, massive wardrobes that looked as though they might have come with the house, even a marble washstand with a bowl and jug.

It was not the most inspiring of rooms and certainly not where she had expected to spend her honeymoon. 'I'll fetch the cases up,' said Jacob cheerfully, and she heard him whistling as he ran down the stairs.

He was content, there was no doubt, but she felt like crying. She hated this house. It had an ominous feel about it. She knew instinctively that she would not be happy here.

CHAPTER FOUR

Surprisingly, during the next few days, Ivory felt more content than she ever had in her life. Jacob was the perfect companion, friend and lover. They tramped for hours over the moors, following well-trodden paths, coming across unexpected outcrops of granite, vast areas of scrubland and heath, yellow gorse, shaggy moorland cattle.

Sometimes there was miles and miles of nothing. Wind and rain had eroded the soil, littering it with granite boulders until there was no beauty left.

In other directions there were gently rolling hills, woods and hedgerows, splashes of colour where wild flowers grew. It was a wild unspoilt part of Cornwall and because Jacob loved it Ivory decided that she loved it too. Not that she would have liked to be there on her own, she wouldn't. It was too lonely a place for that.

Then one afternoon Jacob announced he had some papers he wanted to look through. 'I thought this was our honeymoon, not a working holiday,' she accused sharply.

'It won't take more than an hour,' he said. 'It's something I want to gen up on before we get back.'

'If you consider that more important than me,' Ivory declared petulantly, 'then do it,' and flounced out of the house. She walked for more than half an hour before discovering a pool and sitting near its edge, watching the rings of water as insects alighted on the surface.

It was their first quarrel since that episode over the wine and she knew she had acted childishly and selfishly. But without Jacob what was there to do?

The sun was warm and soporific and Ivory lay back on the spiky grass, closing her eyes and listening to the drone of a bee and the chirrupping of grasshoppers.

She was not aware that she had fallen asleep, not until she looked at her watch some time later and discovered that three hours had gone by. She sprang up. Jacob would be worrying about her! Or would he? Wouldn't he have come after her by now if he had been concerned? More than likely he was still going through those damn papers.

Nevertheless she hurried back, pausing only when she saw a strange car outside the house. She wondered who could be calling in this out of the way place.

The door was open and her sandalled feet made no sound as she entered. She heard the high-pitched sound of a woman's laugh, then a husky sensual voice saying, 'How much longer is your hoydenish wife going to be, Jacob? I can't wait to see whether Rose's description of her is accurate.'

Ivory clenched her teeth in sudden anger. Hoydenish indeed! But when she looked down at her brief cotton shorts and her long coltish legs, and remembered that she had tied her hair into two pigtails, she realised the description could be true.

Then the door to the living room swung open and a young man about Ivory's own age with thick golden hair and friendly blue eyes came out into the hall. He stopped short when he saw

Ivory, glancing admiringly at her tanned trim figure. 'I guess you must be Jake's new bride? I must say you're not what I expected.'

Ivory lifted her chin and wondered who this good-looking boy with the American accent might be. 'Are you disappointed?'

'Heavens, no!' he said at once. 'I'm surprised at Jake for having such good taste and,' he lowered his voice confidentially, 'I wish I'd met you first.'

Ivory smiled, flattered by his flirtatious manner, then the next second went tense as the unknown woman spoke again. 'Who are you talking to, Giles? If it's Jacob's wife bring her in. She's kept us waiting long enough.'

A flicker of apprehension invaded Ivory's stomach, and she wished she had had time to change. It should not matter what anyone else thought, it was Jacob who counted, but because she had made a bad impression on his colleagues she would have liked to appear her best now. Not that this young man seemed to care what she looked like. In fact he seemed to approve.

Inside the room Jacob sat in one of the deep arm-chairs with its faded cretonne cover, a slender woman in her late twenties, with silver-blonde hair and a strikingly beautiful face, perched on the arm. Her eyes were an unusual violet shade, her nose short and straight, her perfect lips emphasised with damson-coloured gloss.

A pale mauve dress clung slavishly to her pointed breasts and rode high over long slender legs that were crossed, one daintily shod foot resting, as though by accident, on Jacob's muscular thigh.

Ivory took in the scene at a glance, feeling as gawky as a schoolgirl in front of this fashionable woman. Jacob sprang to his feet and came across, pulling her against him with all his usual warmth and appreciation, and suddenly she felt better, smiling up into his face, accepting his kiss.

'My love, we were wondering where you had got to?'

'I went for a walk and I'm afraid I fell asleep,' she admitted shyly. 'I'm sorry.'

'Don't apologise,' he muttered thickly. 'I was just afraid you might have fallen and were lying hurt. I was going to come and look for you.'

But you didn't she thought bitterly. You sat here and enjoyed this beautiful woman's company instead. 'I'm all right,' she managed. 'Aren't you going to introduce me?'

'Of course,' he smiled. 'This is Valma Eastland, a very old and very close friend of mine. Valma, Ivory.'

Ivory felt a swift stab of pain and it was all she could do to fix a smile to her lips. So this was the woman who had left her clothes in Jacob's wardrobe, who Rose had said would not be pleased to hear of his marriage? She was every inch as beautiful as she had expected.

'Your child bride? How sweet!' Valma eased herself up from the chair, swinging her hips sexily as she walked towards them, holding out her hand with its long slender fingers, the nails painted purple to match her lips, a ring on each of the fingers.

She barely touched Ivory's hand before she withdrew. 'You're exactly as I imagined, even younger perhaps. I must admit, Jacob, you surprise me. She's not your usual type.'

He smiled lazily. 'Who's to say what is my type, Valma?'

The woman gave an unconcerned shrug, but

Ivory knew what she was thinking. Before she had time to dwell on it, however, Jacob drew her attention to the golden-haired young man who hovered just inside the doorway.

'And this is Giles Mattrell, Ivory.'

Ivory looked across and smiled. 'Hello, Giles.'

'Ivory,' he nodded, and seemed to be having difficulty in taking his eyes off her.

Jacob frowned angrily and turned his back on the boy. 'I think you ought to go and change, Ivory. We're eating out. Valma and Giles are joining us.'

She felt her heart drop, not minding so much that their honeymoon was being interrupted, but the fact that it was this woman who was doing it. The atmosphere would be electric.

It was a relief to get out of the room, and she sat down on the bed for a few minutes, staring at her reflection in the dressing-table mirror. It was no wonder, she thought, that Valma Eastland had not been impressed. There were grass stains on her shirt and dead grass in her hair. In fact not at all a suitable wife for the very wealthy Jacob Pendragon.

Not that Jacob ever complained, and she had worn shorts and skimpy tops every day they had been down here. She saw no point in wearing smart dresses when they spent most of their time on the moors—or in bed!

A flush stained her cheeks and she felt a small measure of triumph. For all her airs and graces Valma had not succeeded in getting Jacob to marry her—and he must have known that this was what the woman wanted.

It was surprising the air of superiority this gave Ivory, and she felt much better as she took a shower and washed her hair, drying it quickly

with her electric dryer, and then leaving it loose
about her shoulders.

She chose a jade-green Chinese-style dress
with silver embroidery. It was one she had not
yet worn and was tasteful without being too old
for her. She matched it with jade eye shadow and
outlined her eyes with a kohl pencil so that they
appeared bigger and more luminous than they
usually were.

She took one last look at herself before going
downstairs and was confident that she looked
nothing at all like the girl who had come in off
the moors.

The high heels of her silver sandals clicked on
the tiled floor of the hall and when she entered
the room all eyes turned in her direction.

Valma frowned.

'Stunning!' said Giles.

Jacob smiled warmly and came across to her.
'My beautiful wife, you've excelled yourself.'

Ivory could not help darting a tiny glance of
triumph in Valma's direction, but recoiled when
she saw the stone-cold hatred on the other
woman's face.

It was gone in an instant. She came across and
said in a voice that must have fooled everyone
except Ivory, 'What a transformation. It seems I
misjudged you.'

'Jacob said proudly, 'Ivory has the rare quality
of being able to switch her personality with the
clothes that she wears. She can be anything from
an ingenue to a siren. It makes life very
interesting.'

Ivory had not realised he had this opinion of
her, but it certainly gave her confidence a boost,
and she observed with satisfaction Valma's
moment of uncertainty.

'If you're ready, my love, we'll go.' He took her arm and Valma followed bad-temperedly, her hand tucked into Giles's arm.

The short drive along the lane to Jamaica Inn was accomplished in silence, but Ivory could feel Valma's hatred and prayed that she need not meet this woman too often.

During the meal Ivory basked in Giles's open admiration, and wondered about his relationship with Valma. They made an odd couple, he being so much younger, and when Valma devoted more of her attention to Jacob than she did her young friend, he wasted no time in talking to Ivory.

His eyes were blue, but not as electric as Jacob's, and there was no other comparison between the two men. Giles was slim and boyish and was pathetically naïve, showing his admiration of her far too openly.

Once or twice she caught Jacob's eyes on them as she and Giles discussed the latest hits in the charts and who were their favourite singers. But each time Valma claimed his attention and apart from his frown of disapproval there was nothing he could say.

Ivory discovered that she had a lot in common with Giles, and he made her laugh, but in no way did he affect her physically as had Jacob on that first meeting.

When they got back to Blackstone it was late and Valma and Giles regretfully said they must get back to the hotel in Bodmin. Valma, having monopolised Jacob for the whole evening, looked as pleased as a cat who has stolen the cream. Giles on the other hand looked regretful and he held Ivory's hand for a second or two longer than was necessary, she herself pulling away when she felt Jacob's eyes upon her.

Once inside he said tersely, 'I don't wish you to have anything to do with Giles. He's a bad lot.'

Ivory was surprised by the vehemence of his attack, but a little angry, too, because he had done nothing to escape from Valma's clutches. 'So what was I supposed to do while you were being claimed by Valma? Sit in silence, ignore Giles? If you ask me she wasn't being very fair on him.'

'He ogled you all evening, and you did nothing to stop him,' he accused. 'Do you think I found that flattering?'

'I expect you felt how I did when you did nothing to stop Valma taking possession of you.' He was being unreasonable.

'Valma is an old friend,' he said tightly. 'There is a difference.'

'Oh, yes,' she drawled. 'Valma had her sights set on you long before I came on the scene, I know that. But since you chose to marry me I think the least you could have done was put her in her place.'

'Are you suggesting that you are jealous of Valma?' he asked incredulously. 'That is ridiculous. Valma's like a sister to me. We're very close, I freely admit that, but there's nothing at all going on between us.'

Ivory eyed him disbelievingly. 'So you keep telling me.'

He shrugged. 'It's true. It was all over a long time ago.'

Not so far as Valma was concerned, thought Ivory, but kept her thoughts to herself. She did not want an argument about Jacob's past girl friends to spoil her honeymoon. 'I'm sorry,' she said softly. 'I didn't mean anything. Giles was so friendly, I couldn't help myself.'

'He's also nearer your own age,' growled Jacob.

And she suddenly realised why he was so disgruntled. 'Oh, Jacob,' she cried, and slid her arms around his waist, holding herself urgently against him. 'Giles is so immature compared to you. I could never think of him in that way.'

He groaned and kissed her with an animal hunger that startled and thrilled her at the same time. 'Hell, I'm sorry,' he said huskily. 'I couldn't help myself. I ought to know you better than that, but I can't help remembering that you once said I was old.'

'You're not, you're not,' she protested. 'I never even notice it now.'

They went to bed and in the darkness Jacob took control of her body and she forgot all about Valma and Giles and everything else. Jacob took her to the heights and they stopped there until she fell asleep.

But Ivory dreamt about Valma. She dreamt the woman took Jacob from her, and the next morning she asked why Valma had come to see them. 'It was not a very nice thing to do on our honeymoon. Couldn't she have waited until we got back?'

He ran the tip of his finger down her nose and across her lips. 'My jealous little wife. Valma is a law unto herself. She's been on holiday these last few months. When she got back and discovered I had married in her absence she decided it was time to pay her parents a visit. They own an hotel in Bodmin. And naturally when she was so close it would have been unsociable not to call on me.' He laughed as he spoke, suggesting he had seen through Valma's explanation. 'Now she's seen you she'll be satisfied, my sweet. Don't worry. She won't interrupt us again.'

'And who is Giles?' asked Ivory. 'Her latest lover?'

'Hell, I hope not,' he gruffed. 'Giles is—well, Giles is Giles. The least you know about him the better.'

Ivory felt dissatisfied with this answer, but knew Jacob well enough by now not to press him further. The two men had clearly known each other for some time because Giles called Jacob 'Jake' with a familiarity that would not be used by a mere acquaintance.

They spent the day tramping across the moor, watching the buzzards circle overhead, following the track of a badger and waiting breathlessly on the off-chance that they might see one. They were doomed to disappointment and eventually decided it was time they made their way home.

She felt very close to Jacob as they walked hand in hand, but contrary to his prediction that Valma would not butt in on their honeymoon again, her car was standing outside the house when they crested the tor that stretched up and away from the house.

Ivory swallowed her disappointment and vowed not to say anything to Jacob, no matter what. She was not jealous of Valma. She was not! But it was all very well telling herself this. The nearer they got to the house the greater grew the lump in her throat.

By the time they reached it she was gripping Jacob's hand so tightly that he could not mistake how deeply her feelings ran. 'I'll tell her,' he said quietly. 'She won't come again, I assure you.'

She gave him a weak smile. 'I know it's not your fault, but I can't help feeling—insecure. She's so lovely and polished and assured. I can't think what you see in me.'

He stopped and held her in front of him. 'When you're Valma's age you'll knock her into

fits. Her appearance has been carefully cultivated,
your beauty is natural. Don't ever doubt yourself,
Ivory. If I'd wanted Valma I could have had her,
as you well know. You were my choice, my love,
and I have no regrets.' He lowered his head and
kissed her tenderly. 'Promise me you'll not let her
bother you?'

Her eyes were moist as she nodded. 'I'll try,
Jacob, but you'll have to help me. I'm not big
and strong like you. I'm weak and a little bit
frightened. I've never had anything to do with
your sort of friends before.'

'You'll learn,' he said confidently.

Valma was already in the house, which they
had left open because Jacob said there was no
need to lock any doors here. She had arranged
herself decoratively in one of the armchairs and
was sipping a glass of Jacob's whisky.

It annoyed Ivory that she had made herself so
very much at home, but heeding Jacob's words
she smiled bravely. 'How nice to see you again,
Valma. You should have let us know you were
coming. I hope we haven't kept you waiting
long?'

'Long enough,' said Valma through clenched
teeth. 'I've brought you an invitation, from my
parents, they'd like you both to dine with them
this evening.'

Ivory felt a flicker of alarm as she glanced
questioningly at her husband, relieved when he
shook his head. 'Sorry, Valma, but it's not on.
We're on honeymoon, remember, and you, my
beautiful friend, are not wanted.'

Valma smiled but her eyes were glacial as they
darted from Jacob to Ivory. She rose with
languid grace, sensuously stretching her long
limbs. 'You disappoint me, Jacob darling. They

won't like it if you go back to London without seeing them.'

'And I don't like it when you keep interrupting Ivory and me,' he said pointedly.

She gave him a long intimate look. 'I understand, but I shall be devastated if you don't look me up when you're back in the city.' She blew him a kiss and sauntered from the room. ''Bye, you two. Mind what you're doing.'

Ivory now knew what it felt like to have an enemy. Although the woman's air had been casually indifferent there was no mistaking her hostility. She hated Ivory's guts like she had hated nothing else in her life.

Ivory shivered, but knew she must put on a front for Jacob's benefit. 'So that's that.' Her voice was distinctly wavery.

'I don't think we'll be seeing her again,' he said gruffly.

But in less than two minutes Valma was back. 'Jacob, my sweet, I can't start the car. Would you have a look at it for me, there's a pet. It's as dead as a dodo.'

Ivory expected Valma to follow Jacob from the room, but instead she remained behind, turning to Ivory immediately he was out of earshot. 'A word of warning, my dear, Jacob's mine. He always has been, and if I have my way he always will be.'

So this hard brittle woman was not going to give up. Ivory stared at her contemptuously. 'Then why didn't he marry you?'

Valma shrugged. 'Foolish me, I've been playing hard to get. I went away on this cruise thinking it would make up his mind for him.' Her face contorted in sudden anger. 'I forgot all about that stupid will.'

'I'm afraid I don't know what you are talking about,' returned Ivory smoothly.

Fine brows arched. 'He didn't tell you? But no, Jacob's too chivalrous for that. He would let you think he was marrying you because he loved you.'

A cold shiver ran down Ivory's spine. She had a feeling that the premonition of disaster she had experienced when first coming to this house was about to explode into hard fact. 'He does love me.' She tried to make her voice strong but there was that touch of uncertainty that made the other woman smile. And now she thought about it, Jacob had never once actually said that he loved her. She had simply taken it for granted.

'Maybe he tells you he does, but Jacob's very good at that. He'll make any woman feel she is his most prized possession.'

'Are you suggesting he had some ulterior motive in marrying me?' Ivory asked with a touch of defiance.

'But of course, my dear.' Long fingers patted an imaginary stray strand of hair into place. 'It was a condition of his father's brother's will that he would not inherit his estate unless he was married by his thirty-fifth birthday. Simple, isn't it?'

Ivory felt the colour drain from her face but refused to believe that this woman was telling the truth.

'I can see you think I'm making it up,' continued Valma, 'but it's true. Jacob's uncle was very fond of him, but deplored the fact that he showed no signs of settling down. His uncle had never married and I think he saw a lot of himself in Jacob. Perhaps he was lonely in his old age and wanted to prevent Jacob making the same mistake. But the stipulation was that unless Jacob married the money would go to his half-brother, even though he was no blood relation. There was simply no one else for him to leave it to.'

'Jacob's a wealthy man in his own right,' protested Ivory. 'Why wouldn't he want his half-brother to have it?'

Valma shrugged airily. 'Some men have an obsession about money. On the other hand he spends it just as easily—and it doesn't last for ever. Even you should know that.'

Too true she did. She knew that Jacob spent money as though it was going out of fashion, and she knew how long she had been saving to buy her own shop, afraid to dip into it, knowing how quickly it would dwindle if she was not careful.

But she could not accept that Jacob had married her for selfish reasons. It just did not make sense. Unless he was a better actor than she gave him credit for?

'Does Jacob's half-brother know about this money?'

'Heavens, no!' Valma looked horrified. 'Can you imagine how he'd react? He would do all he could to stop Jacob marrying. Wouldn't you, if you stood to inherit half a million?'

Ivory swallowed and could think of nothing to say, and Jacob chose that moment to come back into the house. 'I can't find a thing wrong with your car, Valma. It started first time. But I've checked your leads just in case. If you have any more problems I should get it checked over.'

'You're an angel. I don't know what I'd do without you. See you both in London, I expect?' She blew him a kiss and swept from the room.

Ivory shivered and could not meet Jacob's eye. 'I'll make a drink,' she said, and rushed out, relieved when he did not follow. She needed time to think. Valma's surprise statement had shocked her to the core. Although she did not want to believe it, it made sense.

She had never been able to understand why Jacob had married her. It was clear now he had chosen her simply because she *was* naïve. He had expected her to be flattered, to succumb slavishly and ask no questions at all.

Like Valma had said, he enjoyed spending money as much as making it. He had already spent thousands upon herself—and now she knew from where it had come.

She felt suddenly sick.

When the tea was made she carried the tray through to their living room, but her hand shook so much when she poured it that Jacob looked at her questioningly. 'You're not letting Valma's visits upset you?'

Ivory shook her head. 'I don't feel well. I have a bad head.'

At once he was all concern. 'Why didn't you tell me, my love? Let me get you some tablets. Perhaps you ought to go to bed?'

His solicitations, now she knew they were all an act, made her go deathly cold inside. It was all she could do not to turn on him and accuse him outright of marrying her for all the wrong reasons.

But that would get her nowhere. He would deny it until he was blue in the face if necessary. Explaining the position was not a part of his plan. He would wait until she was tired of him. Only last night he had suggested that she might be attracted towards Giles. It was clearly very much to the forefront of his mind that one day she would go. In that way no one would ever guess that he was not the perfect gentleman he purported to be.

'I think I might,' she said at length in a quiet little voice. 'In fact, if you don't mind, I think I'd like to sleep in one of the spare rooms?' She did not think she could bear to sleep with him any more. The thought of physical contact made her cringe.

He frowned. 'I won't wake you when I come up.'

'I wasn't thinking about that,' she grimaced, still avoiding looking directly at him. 'I thought I might keep you awake. I might be sick—I really do feel quite ill.'

She rushed from the room and when he made to follow, 'No, leave me. Please, Jacob, I'd rather be alone.'

He looked uncomfortable but did as she asked, turning back into the room and picking up his cup of tea. 'I'll come up later to see how you are.'

Ivory slowed and her feet dragged as she climbed the stairs. She stripped the dust covers off the furniture in the bedroom next to theirs and without even bothering to undress flung herself down on to the bed, sobbing until she had no tears left. The discovery that Jacob had married her for no other reason than to inherit his uncle's substantial fortune was more than she could take.

How he must have laughed behind her back. How gullible he must have thought her. No doubt the expensive gifts had been to appease his conscience. Had he ever stopped to think what it might do to her if she found out?

Perhaps he had thought there was no chance of that. If so, he had reckoned without Valma. Valma would stop at nothing to make Jacob her man. Ivory could well imagine the shock she must have received when she discovered Jacob had married in her absence. And to someone like Ivory! That must have added insult to injury.

One thing was clear. She could not remain with him any longer. She would conjure up some excuse, something plausible that he would believe. She did not want to suffer the humiliation of admitting that she had discovered the real reason he had married her. Nor could she give herself to him when his feelings for her were no more than a need for physical fulfilment. She was crazy to go on loving him after this monumental discovery and she was bitterly angry with herself for doing so, but it was not a thing she could help.

When Jacob came up a half hour later she was still lying on the bed. Her tears had dried but she had covered her face with her hands as if by so doing she could shut him out.

'Are you asleep?' His hushed voice only just reached her.

Very slowly she lifted her hands and looked at him bleakly.

'You look awful,' he said, and bent down to stroke the hair from her face.

Ivory jerked away and he frowned. 'Have you taken anything for it?'

'No,' she said dully. There was nothing you could take for a broken heart.

'I'll get you some aspirin,' he said and disappeared. A few minutes later he came back with a cup of warm milk and a couple of tablets, then insisted that she get into bed properly. He smoothed fresh sheets into position and then fetched her nightie and stood there while she undressed.

It was an ordeal Ivory would not like to go through again. It seemed positively indecent to stand naked before a man who did not love her, who had used her body mercilessly, had taken what was willingly offered, but who had no real feelings of affection in return.

'If you're not better in the morning,' he added, 'I shall fetch the doctor.'

'I don't think that will be necessary,' managed Ivory shakily, for once glad there was no telephone at Blackstone. Otherwise he would send for him now—and what could she say was wrong with her? 'I think I might sleep now. I'm sorry, Jacob, for being a nuisance.'

And surprisingly this was true. She hated putting him to all this trouble. She hated having to lie. She loved him desperately, agonisingly, was broken only by the fact that he had deceived her.

When Ivory awoke the next morning she felt much better. She had accepted the situation. All that remained now was for her to find a reason to leave.

She ate breakfast which he brought to her on a tray. A boiled egg and some very thin bread and butter, a glass of fresh orange and a pot of tea. He treated her like an invalid, hovering uncertainly until she was ready to scream.

And then, although she had been told she was not wanted, Valma put in another of her appearances. Ivory heard her high voice and quickly got out of bed. She had no wish for this woman to know the devastating effect her revelation had had on her.

When she went down Jacob was looking worried and Valma jubilant. Giles sat quietly on the other side of the room, his face lightening only when Ivory entered.

'Ivory,' said Jacob anxiously, 'would you be all

right if I left you for an hour or so? Valma's
parents have a problem concerning a take-over
bid for their hotel that they want me to sort out. I
told her you're not well, but apparently it won't
wait.'

'I'm fine,' said Ivory at once, smiling bravely.
'Now I'm up my headache's gone. I'll probably
go for a walk. Don't worry about me.' In fact it
was the best thing that could have happened. It
would give her the time she needed to decide
what she must do.

'I'll keep you company,' said Giles at once, his
boyish face lit with enthusiasm. 'Don't worry,
Jake, she'll be safe in my hands.'

Jacob frowned momentarily, then his face
cleared. 'I'd be grateful. I really don't like leaving
her alone.'

Ivory felt choked inside. He was taking the
opportunity to throw them together! The sooner
he got them paired off the sooner he could
conveniently get her out of his hair! It didn't bear
thinking about.

She was convinced that Valma's tale about her
parents needing Jacob's help was nothing more
than an excuse. Valma was eaten away with
jealousy and would stop at nothing to get Jacob
to herself.

Nevertheless Jacob was very convincing. He
asked Ivory time and time again whether she
would be all right, and gave Giles strict
instructions not to let her tire herself. 'In fact, I
think you should stay in,' he said. 'It could be
our long day out yesterday that upset you. Maybe
you've overdone it?'

'Don't fuss, Jacob,' said Ivory irritably. 'Go
and get on with your business.' She chose not to
look at Valma's face.

Not until they had gone did she relax, even then she had to be careful what she said in front of Giles. Not that Giles seemed to notice there was anything wrong. 'I can't believe my luck,' he said. 'Fancy old Jake going off and entrusting his wife to me. Things are looking up.'

'Is there any reason why he shouldn't?' asked Ivory lightly. 'You're not a lecher, or anything like that; are you?'

He grinned, showing a set of very white teeth. 'No such luck. He usually accuses me of being irresponsible, that's all.'

'And are you?' she asked, decidingg that he really was a most attractive boy, and he certainly did not look irresponsible to her. He was young, like herself, with all the careless optimism of youth. Look how blindly she had gone into marriage with Jacob! In fact she would hazard a guess that she and Giles had a lot in common.

'I have my mad moments,' he admitted. 'What teenager doesn't?'

She wondered if she dared ask what his relationship with Valma was. It still appeared to her as most odd. They were always together yet did not act as though they were lovers. 'How long have you known Valma?' she enquired casually after they had set off on their walk.

'All my life, I guess,' he said. 'She was our au pair when I was about six and has come back for a holiday every year since. She struck up a friendship with my brother. I'm surprised he did not marry her. I know it was what she wanted. But enough about Valma, let's make the most of this unexpected opportunity.'

So there was another man in Valma's life! She wondered whether Jacob knew about him. Whether that was one of the reasons why he had

asked her, Ivory, to marry him and not Valma.
Perhaps he had done it to get his own back, as
well as making sure he got the money instead of
his half-brother. She was not so sure now that
she believed him when he said that everything
had been over between them a long time ago. No
man would leave his bride to go and help a
former girl-friend, especially on their honeymoon,
and especially when his wife was not well. Valma
really had him on a string.

She was glad in a way because it made her
decision all the easier. Valma was welcome to a
man whose motives for marriage were personal
gain.

The morning passed more pleasantly than
Ivory had expected. Giles was fun to be with and
they laughed and ran and thoroughly enjoyed
themselves. It was with reluctance that Ivory
eventually suggested they return.

When they got back to the house Jacob and
Valma were already there. Jacob's brow was
black. 'Where the hell have you two been?'

Giles said flippantly, 'Having a good time.
Your wife's a definite stunner, Jake. I can't think
what she sees in an old man like you.'

Livid colour flooded Jacob's face. 'If you've
laid one finger on Ivory, Giles, I swear to God
I'll kill you.'

Ivory had never seen him so angry. He looked
as though he was ready to pounce on Giles. 'For
goodness sake,' she cried quickly. 'We've been
walking, that's all.' Although she was seeking a
way out she had no intention of having a show-
down in front of Valma. But his apparent
jealousy of Giles did give her an idea.

For the moment, though, she felt it necessary
to placate him. There was already a gleam in

Valma's eye, almost as if she had engineered this whole thing—and it was going entirely to plan.

'I thought you were ill,' snarled Jacob.

'I'm better now,' returned Ivory lightly. 'The fresh air did me good.'

'And my company, of course,' added Giles, giving her a conspiratorial wink that must have made it look as though something had gone on between them, even though he had done no more than give her a light peck on the cheek when she had accidentally stumbled against him.

Jacob's mouth tightened. 'I think you'd better go, Giles—and don't bother to come back.'

He shrugged easily. 'I'm in Valma's hands, Jake. I can't go until she's ready.'

'She's only waiting for you,' growled Jacob, and then in a slightly softer tone to Valma, 'I'm glad I could be of some help.'

Her smile, as she rose, held just the right degree of intimacy. 'Thank you, darling. I knew I could rely on you. Come along, Giles, there's a good boy.'

He went with reluctance, turning to look at Ivory with a longing in his eyes that did not go unnoticed by Jacob. When they had gone there was a long silence before he said thickly, 'Now suppose you tell me what went on?'

'Nothing,' said Ivory, in a voice that was deliberately innocent. The success of her plan depended on how she played her part now. If she could make Jacob jealous, hint that she had something to hide, then when the time came for her to say that she was leaving him for Giles it would make it all the easier for him to believe.

'Don't give me that,' he snarled savagely. 'I only have to look at Giles's face to see that he's taken a shine to you.'

'That doesn't mean we did anything,' returned Ivory defensively.

'I know Giles,' he said. 'He thinks he's God's gift to women. He gives me that golden-haired idol sort of rubbish, says the girls can't resist him.'

'He is extremely good looking.'

'And I suppose you fell for his line of patter? You disgust me, Ivory. You're married now, don't forget. You made your choice. Are you regretting it already?'

His attitude annoyed her to such an extent that she spoke without thinking. 'I could be.'

He froze, the cold blue of his eyes fixed relentlessly on her face. 'I hope I did not hear you correctly.'

She eyed him belligerently. 'I'm afraid you did.'

'Hell, I don't believe this,' he cried. 'You can't possibly be attracted to a swine like him.'

Unfortunately, no. Jacob was the swine she was attracted to, who held her heart but had no compunction about using her to further his own ends. So she must have no compunction about using Giles. Not that Giles would mind, he would be tickled pink if he thought he stood a chance of winning her away from Jacob.

'I can't help it,' she said. 'Meeting Giles made me realise that I never really loved you. I find you physically exciting, but that's all. I mistook it for love. I can't cope, Jacob, not with your friends, your business associates, not with you.'

'So what you're trying to tell me is that you want to opt out, now, before it goes any further?' His face was twisted with what looked like pain, but she could not believe this, not when he had married her for selfish reasons alone.

She nodded silently. 'It's for the best.'

'So that you can be free to have your fling with Giles?'

'Yes,' she whispered, unable to meet his eyes as she lied. 'He understands me better than you.' She had not planned this to happen so quickly. She had intended to be more subtle, not realising that Jacob would force her hand.

He looked like a man who had been handed a death sentence. 'You do realise what you would be giving up? Giles hasn't a penny—if he had it would go through his fingers like water. He's no good, Ivory. He never has been, he never will be.'

'And you are, I suppose?' she demanded heatedly. 'I expect you'd deny that all you're interested in is money and the power it gives you? Well, let me tell you something—money doesn't interest me at all. You've tried to buy me—but it hasn't worked. In fact you can have all your gifts back—starting with this.' She wrenched off her rings and threw them at him.

His face became an implacable mask and she quailed beneath the fierceness of his gaze. Then he turned his back and said in a voice entirely devoid of emotion. 'If you walk out on me now, Ivory, don't ever expect to come back into my life.'

'I shouldn't want to,' she thrust bitterly, feeling as though she was bleeding inside. This was the hardest thing she had ever done and she knew she would never forget this moment until her dying day.

His shoulders flinched, as though she had whipped him, but there was nothing on his face to suggest that he was hurt when he swung round. 'Shall I take you to London myself, or would you prefer Giles to do it? It's a wonder he didn't wait. I'm sure you must have discussed this with him.'

'I'll go with Giles,' she said quietly, knowing the long ride with Jacob would kill her. It was best it was over and done with now. There was no point in prolonging the agony. He was letting her go without a fight, and that hurt more than anything else. It proved conclusively that he had no love for her.

Without a word Jacob left the room and she heard tyres scream as he drove from the yard. She broke down in tears, unable to believe that this was the end of all that had promised to be so good.

It took a little while to pull herself together, but she managed to pack her cases before Giles arrived. There was a peculiar mixture of delight and puzzlement on his face. 'Jacob said you wanted me to drive you to London, but he wouldn't tell me why. He said I should know?'

'Where is he now?' asked Ivory flatly.

'With Valma. She insisted he stay. Would you mind telling me what's going on?'

'I'm leaving him,' announced Ivory, smiling tightly when Giles's very beautiful eyes widened. 'And I told him it was because of you.'

This really did astound Giles. He gave a whoop of delight. 'Hell, I wish I could believe it. I take it I'm the scapegoat, but why? What's gone wrong between you?'

'Everything,' said Ivory bitterly. 'I'd like to explain, but—it wouldn't be fair.' Not that Jacob had been very fair to her, but even so she could not blacken his character.

'Well, this really is a turn-up for the books.' Giles sounded very satisfied. 'Whoever thought I'd get one over on my brother like this.'

Ivory looked at him quickly, her mouth falling open with shock. 'Your brother?'

'Half-brother actually,' admitted Giles. 'Don't say he didn't tell you?'

CHAPTER FIVE

It took Ivory a minute or two to get over her shock. So Giles was the man Jacob had swindled out of his inheritance? It was no wonder he had warned her that Giles had not got a penny—he, Jacob, had it all, and this nice boy was left to manage as best he could.

'There's never been any love lost between us,' admitted Giles. 'If the truth's known, he hates my guts.'

'If Jacob hates you,' she said grimly, 'I hate Jacob. Come on, the quicker we get out of here the better.'

Her premonition that this house spelled disaster had come true. She felt stunned and horrified as she helped load her cases into the beige Rover outside. It had been bad enough knowing what Jacob had done, but to discover that it was this innocent boy who had been the victim of his greed was more than she could stomach.

Giles was not the careful driver that Jacob was, taking unnecessary risks when overtaking and never once keeping to the speed limits imposed. 'Giles,' she said, when they had had a particularly close shave, 'I might want to get away from Jacob, but I don't want to get myself killed. Would you mind slowing down?'

'Sorry,' he grinned ruefully. 'I guess you're right. Valma's parents would never forgive me if I crashed their car.'

'It's not yours then?' She ought to have known.

It was not the type a young American would own.

'Hell, no. Mine's a T Bird, but it's back home in L.A. The Eastlands always let me use one of theirs when I'm over here.'

'All the more reason you should be careful,' she returned primly.

After that he took it steady but Ivory could see that he was not happy about it. She guessed he liked to live dangerously. She could imagine him whooping it up around his home town, attracting all the girls with his devil-may-care attitude. He probably had not been kidding when he told Jacob they could not resist him.

Her Aunt Eleanor was appalled when she discovered that Ivory had left Jacob. 'My dear child, you've not given yourself time. And who is this?' She looked accusingly at Giles, clearly of the opinion that he was the one who had stolen her from her husband.

'This is Giles Mattrell, Jacob's half-brother,' explained Ivory. 'He's kindly brought me home.'

'I see.' But her lips were prim. 'I take it he interrupted your honeymoon?'

'You could say that,' she replied carefully, 'but if you don't mind I'd rather not answer any questions now. Do you think you could find Giles some food before he returns to Cornwall?'

But Giles smiled easily and held up his hand. 'No need, Auntie dear. I think I might spend a couple of nights in London. I'll go and find myself an hotel. Perhaps I'll be seeing you, Ivory?'

'I doubt it,' she returned tightly. 'I'm going to hibernate. But thanks for helping me out.'

He grinned. 'Don't let him get you down, girl. Don't forget I've had years of experience dealing with Jake. The only way to win with him is not to let him see that he bothers you.'

He certainly did not look as though he cared. Ivory wondered whether he would be so flippant and uncaring if he knew about the money he could have inherited but hadn't. She guessed he would not look at Jacob so tolerantly then.

Quite how she got through the next few weeks Ivory did not know. She received a letter from Jacob's lawyers offering her a very generous allowance, but she wrote back at once, stating in no uncertain terms that she wanted nothing at all from him. She returned the car, and all the jewellery and clothes he had bought her she dumped in his apartment, leaving her key on top.

This ought to have severed all connections, but there was still the question of her heart. She could do nothing at all about that. It was crazy to go on loving a man who had used you, who had deliberately and cold-heartedly set out to marry you for reasons that had nothing at all to do with loving and caring. God, how he had fooled her. Never for one moment had she doubted his sincerity.

She recalled with startling clarity the day she had promised to marry him. He had kissed her in front of her aunt, saying hoarsely, 'Don't let me down now, little one. I need you like I've never needed anyone else in my whole life.' Now she knew why!

At least she had Valma to thank for opening her eyes. The crunch when it finally came would have been so much harder to bear if they had been married for any longer.

He was back in London, she knew that. He was in the news when he expressed an interest in the property market. It was his intention, he said, to buy up old and delapidated stately homes and renovate them to their former glory. No doubt making a huge profit for himself into the bargain, thought Ivory bitterly.

The weeks passed slowly, but then her aunt came up with a proposition that pushed all thoughts of Jacob from her mind, exciting and stimulating her, and bringing life back into her numb limbs.

'I've been thinking,' said Eleanor. 'When I die my savings will come to you. I've not got much, a couple of thousand, but if you're still interested in opening that boutique you were always on about, then you might as well have it now. I can manage on my pension, I don't need it. It won't be enough, I know, but I could remortgage the house. What do you think?'

'You'd do that, for me?' Ivory was overwhelmed and had difficulty in holding back her tears.

'I don't like to see you unhappy, child. I feel partly to blame. I should have gone along with my first impression that Jacob was not your type and put my foot down.'

Ivory had never told her aunt the real reason she had left Jacob, just that she found it impossible to reconcile the difference in their ages and lifestyle.

And so Ivory opened her boutique. But although she was full of enthusiasm and optimisim she discovered it was not so easy as she had thought. She was not experienced enough when it came to buying and more than once made the wrong decision. She was left with racks of dresses that no one wanted, and was compelled eventually to sell them off at below cost simply to cut her losses.

Competition all around her was keen, and although she did her best it soon became apparent that this was not good enough. By the end of two years she was so deeply in debt that she lay awake at night worrying about it.

She was afraid to tell her aunt, always putting on a brave face, saying things were better than they were. In the end not only was her shop in jeopardy but her aunt's house as well.

Finally she was threatened with bankruptcy. It meant losing the shop, her aunt's house, everything, to pay the outstanding debts. How could she tell her aunt this? Where would they live? She had failed to live up to her aunt's faith in her. She had let her down. She felt almost suicidal.

Irrationally she blamed Jacob. If she had not met and married him none of this would have happened. Then it occurred to her that he was the one person who could help her out of this mess, but she put the thought from her the second it occurred.

She could not possibly ask him for money, not after the way she had accused him of trying to buy her. Money meant nothing to her, she had said. Yet right at this moment it meant the difference between being destitute or carrying on without her aunt finding out about the mess she had got them in to.

Her aunt had not been well lately. A heart murmur, nothing more the doctor had said, a warning to take things easy. And so she had given up her committees and her charity work and spent most of her time at home.

It would finish her if she was thrown out. Ivory could not do it. Asking Jacob for help was the only solution.

She told Eleanor she had a date that evening. She was taking a chance that Jacob would be in, but had decided against phoning first. She did not want him to be prepared.

Her stone-coloured crepe suit was belted neatly at the waist, the skirt slim and elegant. She teamed it with a dark-brown blouse and wore high-heeled matching shoes. She swept her hair up on top and fixed heavy amber earrings to her ears.

She certainly looked older and more confident than the girl he had married. In fact she appeared very cool and calm and no one would guess at the raw emotions avalanching through her stomach. This was exactly the impression she wanted to create. No way did she wish Jacob to guess that she still ached with an hungry love that had never been assuaged.

There had been no one since Jacob. She had seen Giles a few times on his occasional trips to England, and although he would have been prepared to entertain a more serious relationship she had always kept him at arm's length.

Compared to Jacob he was very immature, or was it that she felt so much older for her years? There was only twelve months difference between herself and Giles yet she always felt so much wiser than him. It was her marriage to Jacob that had done this to her, that and her unsuccessful attempts to be a business woman.

She felt almost middle-aged. So much had happened during these last two years. More than happened to most people in a lifetime.

It was not until she stood outside Jacob's door, her heart clamouring loud enough to disturb all the residents in the building, that she realised the folly of coming unannounced.

Her hand was poised on the bell, her mind debating whether to go away and telephone instead, when the door opened and her decision was made for her.

'Well, well, just look who we have here.'

Valma's dulcet tones were the last thing Ivory wanted to hear. But there was no turning back now. She lifted her chin almost imperceptibly and pinning a smile to her lips said in a voice that surprised her by its coolness, 'Hello, Valma, Jacob.'

He stood an inch or two behind her, much taller and broader than she remembered, a swift frown pleating his brow. He inclined his head in acknowledgement but said nothing.

'I'd like a word with you, if I may,' she said quietly.

Valma's fine brows slid smoothly upwards. 'What a pity I haven't time to stop and listen. I'm sure I'd find it most interesting. You'll have to fill me in when I come back from America, darling.' She dropped a lingering kiss on his cheek. ''Bye for now.' Giving Ivory a questing and faintly warning look she tottered on her ridiculously high heels down the corridor.

Jacob stood back, still without speaking, and Ivory moved into his apartment, feeling for all the world like a mouse entering a lion's den. After two years she had forgotten how overpowering he was, how devastatingly male, how physically exciting.

'A drink?' The invitation was such as he might extend to anyone who had called unexpectedly.

She nodded and swallowed a constricting lump in her throat, conscious that the compelling force that had drawn her to him in the first place had in no way diminished. On the way here she had rehearsed all that she was going to say. Now she could remember none of it. All she could do was look at him with hungry eyes, achingly aware of a violent need for this man.

He filled two glasses with whisky and she watched his strong brown hands, recalling the feel of them on her body. When he handed her her drink she almost knocked it flying as his fingers accidentally touched hers.

His face was more gaunt than she remembered, high cheek bones prominent, his square jaw well defined. There were shadows beneath his eyes, lines scored from nose to chin, and a permanent furrow between his brows as though he was in a constant black mood. 'Sit down,' he said.

She obeyed gladly, while he stood tall, silent and aloof, waiting for her to speak. She felt as though he was a stranger. 'You haven't changed,' she managed to whisper after she had taken a sip of the fiery liquid.

'I can't believe you've come here to tell me that,' he said coldly, those blue eyes as glacial as ever they had been, only a muscle jerking in his jaw telling her that he was not as undisturbed as he pretended to be.

'No,' she admitted, but how on earth was she going to ask him for money? He was giving her no encouragement, not that she had expected any. But he might at least have made a pretence of being pleased to see her. 'I—I need your help, Jacob.'

The thick brows shot up. 'What makes you think I'll be prepared to give it?'

'I don't,' she said throatily, wishing he would make it easier. 'I wouldn't ask you—if it was for myself—but it's my aunt, you see. I . . .'

She did not know how to go on. He was like a

statue chiselled out of granite, formidable, unrelenting. She felt close to tears.

'Your aunt needs my help. In what way?' The deep timbre of his voice vibrated in that room, making her shiver and wrap her arms about herself.

'She doesn't know I'm here, of course. In fact—she—doesn't even know that—she's—in trouble.' She stopped and wrung her hands together. She was making a mess of this. She wished she had not come. There must have been some other way. Jacob would not help her. He took money, not handed it out. She was a fool to even think that he might.

He said impatiently, 'For God's sake, Ivory, pull yourself together and get to the point. I haven't got all night.'

There had been a period when he had been prepared to spend every minute of his time with her. When cultivating her had been no trouble at all. Now he had no further interest. She had served her purpose, more than likely doing him a favour by walking out before he decided to get rid of her.

'I need some money,' she husked, and it was the most difficult thing she had ever had to say in her life.

There was a long silence during which she was afraid to look at him. When she did manage to raise her lids there was a gleam in his eyes that frightened her, and more than ever she wished there had been some other way of raising this cash.

'Two years ago you told me in no uncertain terms that you despised money. In fact you seemed to think I was some sick sort of character because I enjoyed making it. Now you have the nerve to come here and ask for some. Christ, Ivory, you don't really expect me to say yes?'

His electric blue eyes were fixed on her face, powerful and hypnotic, pinning her to her seat so that she could not move even though she wanted to.

She found it difficult to breathe and twisted her fingers nervously round the stem of her glass, taking a quick gulp and then choking as it went down the wrong way.

There were tears in her eyes now and she saw Jacob through a blur, but it did not disguise the disgust on his face, his contempt that she had stooped so low as to beg for money. She wished she could walk out and never see him again.

But the force of his gaze was such that all she could do was sit and wait for him to go on. Even a nod that, yes, this was the reason she had come to see him, was more than she could manage.

'I've waited for the day I would see you again, Ivory, but never did I imagine it would be under circumstances like this. God, you must have swallowed some pride to bring yourself here, but it is nothing compared to the hell you put me through when you walked out—or the hell I intend putting you through *if* I help you now.'

She swallowed painfully and summoned up the strength to move, feeling almost as though she had to prise herself from the chair, her limbs leaden, her heart heavy. 'I'm sorry to have troubled you,' she managed to husk. 'It was a mistake. I'll go.'

'Sit down, damn you!' He pushed her none too gently back on to the seat. 'Now you're here you may as well tell me what you want it for.'

She looked down at her lap. 'My—aunt's about to—lose—her home.' Her voice was little more than a whisper.

'Why? What's she been doing?'

Ivory shook her head, still refusing to look at him, noting inconsequentially how well-polished his shoes were. You could almost see your face in them. 'It's my fault. W-when I—left you—she—she gave me all her savings—and re-mortgaged her house—so that I could open my own shop.'

'At eighteen?' he exclaimed incredulously. 'She needs her head examining. And now you've gone bust? I'm not surprised. You're about as business-minded as that idiot half-brother of mine. Did he have anything to do with it?' This last question was asked sharply.

'No,' she whispered miserably.

'I still don't see why this should concern Eleanor. If the business is in your name they can't touch her.'

She risked looking at him. 'It wasn't. It was in her name—we thought it best—because—I was—so young. But she had nothing to do with any of it. She left it all to me. I'm afraid I haven't been paying the bills. Her mortgage, nothing. I couldn't. And they're threatening to take everything to pay the creditors.' She swallowed and continued quickly before she lost confidence altogether. 'My aunt's developed heart trouble, you see, so I daren't tell her. You've no idea how worried I've been these last months.'

He surveyed her with a damning coldness that only he was capable of. 'You really have bitten off more than you can chew. What makes you think I'd be prepared to help? The way you treated me you deserve nothing more than to be shown the door.'

Ivory clenched her teeth and pushed herself up yet again. 'I should have known better. Your

interest is in making money—not handing it out.'
Her voice was savage as well as bitter.

'That's a very damning statement.' The glitter
in his eyes hardened and he seemed to have
momentarily stopped breathing. 'I never kept you
short of anything. In fact I would say I was far
too generous. It was not pleasant having it flung
back in my face.'

'No more than you deserved,' she thrust, not
caring now what she said. It was clear he had no
intention of helping.

'Lord knows what you mean by that cryptic
comment,' he ground, 'but I won't go into that
now. If you want my help, though, I would
advise you to be careful what you say.'

She swallowed jerkily, and although more than
anything she wanted to leave, she had to put her
aunt, not herself, first. 'Does that mean?' she
husked, 'that you would be prepared to lend me
the money?'

'I might,' he said. 'What sort of figure are you
looking for?'

'Thirty thousand.' Her words were hardly
audible, her eyes fixed anxiously on his lean face.

It gave nothing away. 'You certainly don't do
things by halves.'

She had no idea whether he was shocked by the
figure or whether sums like that were chicken
feed to a man of his means. When he could afford
to do deals involving millions, thirty thousand
must seem an infinitesimal amount.

'There'll be conditions,' he continued firmly.

Ivory sat down, her relief so great because at
least he wasn't refusing her outright, that her
legs would no longer hold her. 'I'll agree to
anything,' she said profoundly, 'so long as my
aunt isn't thrown out of her house.' When she

thought of all her aunt had done for her,
humbling herself in front of this man was a
very small thing to do, worth all the distress he
was causing.

'Good,' he said crisply. 'First of all, I'll wind
up your business affairs myself. That way I shall
be sure everything is dealt with satisfactorily and
that no one, because you are young and innocent,
does you out of anything. Secondly, you are to
come and live with me.'

'No, never!' She would not be used by him
again. 'I can't do that, Jacob, you're asking the
impossible.'

'Then it's no deal,' he returned savagely. 'You
may as well go.'

'I can't see the point,' she argued. 'You told me
when I walked out on you that you never wanted
me back in your life.'

'The circumstances have changed.' His tone
was brisk, business-like. 'You would be doing me
a favour—and a very small one compared to the
one you are asking me. It so happens I have
several important business conferences coming
up and I shall be doing a considerable amount of
entertaining, and with Valma away—she's been
offered a job in America which she would be
foolish not to take—I need—'

'A hostess,' cut in Ivory sarcastically. 'Is that
all you would want me for?'

'No,' he snapped sharply. 'That would hardly
be repayment. I would expect you to resume your
position as my wife—in every respect.'

Her cheeks coloured. 'No, Jacob, I couldn't.'

'Why the hell not?' he snarled. 'The way I look
at it it's a very small price to pay.'

Giving herself to a man who did not love her,
small? It would be the most difficult task she had

ever been asked to do. Knowing he did not love her, knowing he was only using her body, getting out of it a selfish satisfaction, it would be humiliation beyond compare.

But what other choice had she? Were Aunt Eleanor's health and home comforts of more concern than her own peace of mind? Of course not. Jacob was right. It was a small price to pay. She had got herself into this mess by trying to run a business when she was not old enough or wise enough to handle it, therefore she had to pay the consequences. Aunt Eleanor must never know how serious things had become.

At least her aunt would be pleased that she had gone back to Jacob, and if the shop was sold and her mortgage repaid she would see nothing unusual in that. As Jacob's wife Ivory would have no need to work. Ivory was thankful she had never told her aunt the true facts.

'I don't seem to have much choice,' she said in a quiet little voice.

'Not if you want the money,' he snapped.

'How long would you expect me to live with you?' she ventured next. 'How long before you would consider the debt paid? I would like to be able to pay it back in hard cash, but if I'm not working that would be impossible.'

'For as long as I want you,' he replied carelessly. 'You're my legal wife, Ivory, don't ever forget that. Now, the third condition.'

Ivory's head jerked and she wondered what was coming next.

'You're to stop seeing Giles. In future he has no part in your life. Is that clear?'

Ivory almost felt like laughing, her relief was so great. 'What makes you think I am still seeing him?'

He eyed her coldly. 'Don't give me that. Giles himself has admitted it, though what you can see in that little worm I have no idea.'

Ivory did not know that Giles still kept up the pretence that they were lovers, although she guessed he would be doing it as much for his own sake as hers. It would give him a feeling of superiority to brag that he had taken Jacob's wife from him.

The least comforting thought about all this was that Jacob had done nothing at all to stop him. It went to show that there had been no feelings at all on his part—it had all been one big act.

On the rare occasions that Giles had taken her out she had discovered that Jacob's opinion of his half-brother was unfortunately only too well founded. He never had any money, even though he had once admitted that his parents gave him a generous allowance. He liked to gamble, he told her, and had tried to encourage her to have a flutter on the horses, or participate in a game of roulette when he had taken her to some nightclub.

But always Ivory had declined. She was of the opinion that it was throwing good money away, could never really understand anyone risking so much on the off-chance that they might win a fortune. The odds were against them every time.

'I can't promise that Giles won't attempt to see me,' she said.

His lips firmed. 'I'll see that he doesn't. You'd better give me the address of your shop. I'll meet you there in the morning. Once I've got the picture I'll take over and do whatever is necessary. And tell your aunt you're coming back to me. If she's not well enough to be left alone I'll see that she gets a nurse to live in.'

His generosity could not be denied, although she could not help wondering how many other people he had conned, simply to make money out of them. She decided she did not trust Jacob at all. It was not nice, to distrust one's own husband, but that was the way it was.

'That won't be necessary,' she said, walking towards the door. 'I shall call in to see her each day, with your permission, of course?'

Jacob frowned, but merely said, 'I'll take you home,' and crossed the room with her.

'That won't be necessary,' she said tightly.

'Allow me to be the judge of that.'

They reached the door together, his hand coming down on top of hers as she wrestled with the handle. She turned to look up at him and for a few tense seconds her eyes were locked into his in a dry-mouthed sort of suspension.

She knew he was going to kiss her even before he made a move, and there was nothing at all she could do about it. Her heart-beats quickened and she felt sure she could hear the throb of Jacob's own heart as he bent his head.

There was something savage and brutal about his kiss, his teeth grinding mercilessly against hers, bruising her lips. It lasted no more than a few seconds, yet the impact made Ivory's head spin.

'What was that for?' she demanded angrily.

'To remind you that you're still my wife.'

'A promise of things to come?' she asked bitterly. 'Let me tell you this, Jacob, you'll get nothing freely.'

There was no denying that despite everything she was still attracted to his strong masculinity. He was a compelling force and it was going to be sheer hell living with him, loving him, all the time knowing that he did not love her. That he never had, that she had been a mere instrument in the game of power that he played.

But because she loved him it did not mean that she was going to make everything easy for him. He must never know how she felt. It was bad enough knowing that he intended to violate her body when he cared nothing for her. He would certainly be making her pay for the favour she had asked.

'Then if I have to rape you, I will,' he returned angrily, his eyes more icily blue than she ever remembered. 'Because I have no intention of being deprived of my conjugal rights.'

He snatched open the door and Ivory made her way out, head held high, lips clamped tightly together. During the drive home neither of them spoke, but Ivory was intensely aware of Jacob. It was as though the long months of being apart had increased rather than diminished her love, and she ached with a desperate kind of longing to be held in his arms, to be loved by him, genuinely loved, not a physical need that any woman could take care of.

He left her outside her aunt's house. Ivory had been afraid he might demand to come in, but apart from a curt confirmation that he would see her at the boutique the next morning he said nothing.

There was a tight-lipped grimness about him that she found threatening and she could not help wondering whether she had done the right thing. But when she got indoors and found her aunt in bed not feeling too good, she knew she had taken the wisest course.

She waited until the following morning before telling Eleanor that she had met Jacob again.

'He's asked me to go back to him,' she admitted quietly, feeling guilty at the small deception.

But her aunt did not even notice. 'This is wonderful news, Ivory. It's what I've hoped and prayed for. Jacob is such a good man, and now that you're older and more confident I'm quite sure you'll be able to cope.'

'I hope so,' said Ivory. 'It will mean selling the shop, of course.'

'I should think so,' replied Eleanor strongly. 'Jacob would not want his wife to work. There'd be no need, would there? Oh, my love, I'm so happy for you.' She took Ivory's hands into her own, her genuine pleasure shining in her eyes.

'I don't really like leaving you, though. If anything—'

'Nonsense,' interrupted her aunt strongly. 'With you happily back with Jacob I'll have no worries. I don't mind telling you now that I did worry about you. I worried a lot. I hate to see marriages breaking up and I don't think you gave yours a fair chance. I'm quite sure Jacob was broken-hearted. But you'll be all right now, I know you will. When am I going to see him again?'

'He's coming to the shop this morning,' admitted Ivory. 'He's going to sort everything out for me, and then we'll come back here for my cases.' She swallowed convulsively. 'It will be strange, going back to him after all this time.'

It felt strange when he walked into the boutique. Although she was prepared for him she had not realised quite the effect he would have on her. He was still by far the most striking man she had ever met, and she wondered how she could have been so foolish as to once think he had fallen in love with her. With his wealth and looks he could have his pick of any woman.

She had simply been the gullible fool he had been seeking—and look where it had got her. She was completely at his mercy now—and there was not one thing she could do about it.

He was brisk and business-like and within hours all her problems were resolved. She could not help but admire the way he worked. Bills were paid, the sale of the shop organised, and even a temporary manager installed to take over the day to day running of the business until such time as it was sold.

'Right,' he said at length. 'We'll collect your cases. You have told your aunt where you're going?'

She nodded. His efficiency had numbed her. She had stood around in a daze and watched as he worked, answering his questions, amazed how astute he was. She had never seen him in action before, but could easily see how he had got where he was. He was dynamic. There was no other word for it.

Eleanor greeted Jacob enthusiastically. He kissed her brow gently and enquired after her health. 'I understand you've not been well? If you'd like a nurse to come in now I'm taking Ivory from you again, I'll be more than pleased to fix it.'

The woman smiled and shook her head. 'It was worry that was doing it. I knew Ivory had made the wrong decision in leaving you, but I also knew it was no good me saying anything. I just hoped she'd come to her senses. I'm glad she has. I know you two are made for each other.'

'You really think so?' He beamed at her, at the same time draping his arm about Ivory's shoulders. 'You see, my restless little wife, your aunt knows better than you.'

He smiled down at her tenderly and Ivory marvelled at his duplicity. She tried to smile in return but it was as much as she could do to look at him. The enormity of what she was about to do weighed heavily on her shoulders.

They stayed for half an hour, Jacob and her aunt chatting while she made a pot of tea, and then all too soon they were on their way to his apartment.

Ivory sat in frozen silence, her hands clasped tightly together, not daring to think what was going to happen when they got there. She could not bear the thought of Jacob making love to her, and she made up her mind not to give in to him, ever. It would not be worth the agony it caused.

Consequently she was as tense as a guitar string when they arrived, flinching when Jacob accidentally brushed against her in the lift which whisked them at high speed to his penthouse apartment. He frowned angrily but said nothing and when they entered he went straight to their bedroom with her cases.

Ivory had been hoping he might relent and give her her own room, and her spirits dropped as she slowly followed him. He flicked open the lids and then left her to unpack while he took a shower. She wished he would speak. This unnatural silence did not bode well for the time they must spend together.

She hung away her clothes, noting grimly that all the new things she had flung back at him were returned to the wardrobe. Had he expected her to return? Or were they there for the use of any girl whom he might invite to his flat? Valma included.

She was still surveying them bitterly when he came back into the bedroom, a towel wrapped about his loins, his black hair flat and wet over his well-shaped head, his eyes enigmatic. 'They're still there.'

'So I see,' she returned quietly. 'Why?'

'Because I knew you'd come back.'

'You couldn't have known I'd need your help,' she cried, swinging round and eyeing him angrily. 'And if I hadn't, no one on earth would have made me.'

'When you'd tired of Giles you would,' he said thickly.

Ivory compressed her lips. 'If you don't mind I'd rather not talk about Giles.'

'Neither would I,' he snarled. 'Do you want a shower before we—resume our married life?'

There was no mistaking what he meant and Ivory turned away in disgust even though the notion of Jacob making love to her was the headiest thought she had had in a long time. There was no disputing that she had missed him. She had lain awake at night longing to feel his arms about her, aching for the satisfaction that he alone could give.

Now that the time had come she no longer wanted him. Not at the expense of Jacob taking her for purely selfish reasons. She spent as long as she could in the shower but in the end knew she must go and face him.

She pulled on a towelling robe and walked with leaden feet into the bedroom. 'I was about to come and fetch you.' Jacob lay on the bed completely naked, but as he spoke he jumped up and came towards her.

Ivory felt her nerves skittering and she eyed him hostilely. 'If you want anything from me, Jacob Pendragon, you'll have to take it by force. I've not changed my mind.'

'In that case,' he said softly, 'it will be my pleasure to change it for you.'

She shook her head wildly as his big hands came down on her shoulders, lifting the robe and sliding it backwards so that it fell to the floor before she could do anything about it.

Then he held her at arm's length and slid his eyes over her in a long intimate appraisal. Ivory grew hot, but was determined not to let him see that he in any way affected her.

'You're as beautiful as I remember,' he said huskily.

'And you're as despicable,' she rasped.

His mouth firmed and he pulled her roughly against him so that she felt the hard muscles pressing against her soft flesh, and inhaled the fresh musky odour of his body. Of their own volition her pulses raced and her heart clamoured, but she was still determined not to give in.

His mouth seized on hers with every intention of inflicting pain, her body was crushed until all the air was driven from her lungs, but she stood still and resolute in his arms, suffering his embrace, but giving nothing at all in return.

'Damn you,' he grated, 'I want a flesh and blood woman not a statue.'

'Then you've picked the wrong person,' she hissed. 'It's not my choice that I'm here.'

'It was your decision to beg me for help. This is your way of repaying me, so respond, damn you. I won't believe that you're completely immune.'

He attacked her mouth again, though this time his tactics were different. Instead of the animal-like hunger with which he had devoured her, his lips gentled, his hands moved with deliberate sensuality over her back and her hips, pulling her resisting body against him until she would have had to be made of stone to ignore his need of her.

All the old familiar feelings flooded back and she knew that her capitulation was inevitable.

CHAPTER SIX

THE aftermath of Jacob's lovemaking left Ivory weak, vulnerable and decidedly unsure of herself. What had happened to her resolution? What power did Jacob possess which made her unable to control her own feelings?

When she felt the pillow damp beneath her cheek she realised that she was crying, and angry with herself she turned her back on Jacob, experiencing a shock when he pulled her roughly over to face him.

His eyes narrowed when he saw the sheen of tears but he made no reference to her distress, saying strongly, 'Don't turn away from me, girl, or you'll regret it.'

Ivory flinched at the hardness of his tone. 'I already regret the day I met you.' He had control of her body, whether she liked it or not, but she was determined he should not have control of her mind.

'You don't mean that.' His hands gripped her shoulders, pressing her back against the bed, his handsome face contorted with rage.

'Don't I?' Ivory eyed him boldly, ignoring the quiver of apprehension which raced through her limbs. 'You don't know anything. I despise everything you stand for.'

'You didn't give me that impression just now,' he snarled. 'In fact I would say you enjoyed every minute of it.'

Ivory shook her head wildly, her beautiful wide eyes full of pain. 'I can't help the way my body behaves, but I swear to you, Jacob, that it means nothing. Nothing, do you hear? Nothing at all.'

He looked at her disbelievingly. 'I'm sorry, Ivory, but you don't convince me. If you truly hated me your skin would crawl when I touch you.'

'And how do you know it doesn't?' she enquired crossly.

'Because I know you well enough to tell whether you're faking or sincere. The way you responded to me told me that you're a woman who's been starved of love for a long time. Didn't my brother please you? Is that why you were so ready to give him up?'

'Giles has nothing to do with my feelings for you,' she declared loudly. 'Let's leave him out of it.'

'Since he was the reason you left me I don't see how we can discount him. Was he a disappointment, Ivory?'

His blue eyes had never been more intense. There was a manic quality about them as they fixed on her face and Ivory felt her throat go dry as she shrank away from the fierceness of his glare.

'Giles never disappointed me,' she declared truthfully. But contrary to what Jacob believed there had been nothing at all between them.

She was unprepared when Jacob shook her violently. 'Don't lie to me,' he grated. 'He has no idea of a woman's needs.'

'At least he never forced himself on me.'

His brow darkened. 'Are you suggesting that I did?'

'Yes,' she cried defiantly. 'You knew that in the end I'd give in. I hate you, Jacob. I really do.' Fresh tears sprang to her eyes.

With a snarl of disgust Jacob flung her from him and for the rest of the night he kept strictly to his side of the bed. Ivory could not sleep a wink. How could she, knowing what this man could do to her?

It was wrong that he should affect her in such a way when all he was doing was using her. He had used her from the very beginning, although she had been too naïve to see through him then. Now she knew exactly where she stood and it sickened her that there was nothing at all she could do about it.

Dawn was breaking when Ivory finally fell asleep and when she awoke Jacob had gone. She lay for a minute staring at the indented pillow, experiencing a curious breathlessness, a quickening of the pulses.

It was the most cruel thing Jacob could have done, she decided, asking her to live with him. It would be sheer hell, knowing that all he was getting out of it was physical satisfaction, with none of the inner contentment that came when two people truly loved each other.

She thought about Valma, and her mouth tightened when it occurred to her that she had probably lain in this very bed. With a strangled cry she jumped out and crossing to the bathroom spent several long minutes beneath the shower's soothing jets, figuratively washing Valma out of her hair.

Not that it succeeded. Valma's personality was stamped everywhere. Her clothes in the wardrobe, perfume on the dresser, a brand new picture in the lounge which could certainly not have been Jacob's choice. It was abstract art at the extreme and whichever way Ivory looked at it it made no sense.

Mrs Humphrey arrived at eleven and beamed her pleasure at seeing Ivory again. 'Mrs Pendragon, you're back! This time for good, I hope? A little bit young you were to be thrown into marriage. Jacob shouldn't have rushed you. But that's what men are like, isn't it? Impatient, I mean. Perhaps frightened that someone else might snap you up, you being so young and beautiful.'

'I don't think that was his idea,' said Ivory bitterly, then decided she had better not say too much in front of this woman, who clearly adored her employer. If she, Ivory, so much as hinted that Jacob had married her simply to get his hands on his late uncle's fortune Humphrey would be up in arms immediately, probably telling Jacob himself what she had said. That would not do at all. Using Giles had been her way of saving face. It would be too humiliating by far to admit that she knew Jacob had married her for mercenary reasons alone. 'But I agree I wasn't ready for marriage.'

'And now you are,' offered the woman. 'I'm so pleased. I can't stand that hoity-toity Valma Eastland, and if the truth's known I don't think Jacob is too taken with her either.'

'Has she—been living here—while I've been away?' Ivory swallowed nervously.

'Heavens no, love, although given half a chance I'm quite sure she'd have been eager to move in. She helps Jacob entertain, that's all, a man needs a woman for that sort of thing. But most of the time he's been here alone. Brooding, if you ask me. Too proud to ask you to come back, but missing you all the same.'

Privately Ivory doubted that. Her leaving him had saved him the bother of getting rid of her.

Mrs Humphrey took her bag through to the kitchen and Ivory followed, and there on the breakfast bar, propped up against the sugar basin, was a note from Jacob.

It informed that he would be bringing back two very important clients that evening and requested that she look her best.

'Hmph!' grunted Humphrey. 'He's certainly lost no time. He could have given you a day or two to settle in.'

It's what I'm here for, thought Ivory, even though she privately agreed. 'I'm used to meeting people now,' she said. 'I have no worries about coping.'

'That's good to hear.' Humphrey filled the kettle and made them both a cup of tea, insisting that Ivory try one of the iced buns she had brought with her. 'You've lost weight,' she accused. 'It's not good for a young girl to be so thin.'

Not until she tried on some of her old dresses did Ivory realise that Mrs Humphrey had observed her keenly. Nothing fitted properly. If she wanted to impress Jacob's clients then it meant a new dress.

She had finished her purchases and was enjoying a well-earned cup of coffee in a popular restaurant when a hand touched her shoulder and Giles's very American voice enquired whether he might join her.

'Need you ask?' she smiled. 'You're what I need right at this moment.'

'Not according to Jake.' The full lips curled in a wry smile as he slid into the seat opposite. 'I've had my orders to keep strictly away. What's going on between you two? Is my role of ardent lover finished?'

'I'm afraid so, Giles,' she said ruefully. 'I'd like to thank you for all you've done. It was a great help.'

He ordered his coffee and a plate of sandwiches. 'Think nothing of it. The pleasure was mine. What I can't believe is that you've gone back to him. I rather gathered you'd left him for good.'

Ivory grimaced. 'I thought I had, but, well, something cropped up, and—we're living together again.'

'I suppose that means you love the guy? How I wish it was me. You never really gave me a chance, did you?' His dark blue eyes were earnest for once.

'Is that what you expected?' she asked. 'I didn't know. I'm sorry, Giles.'

His wide mouth pulled into a crooked smile and he shrugged. 'I guess I always knew you were hooked on Jake. I can't say I admire your taste, but if that's what you want, then I hope things turn out. Don't think you've seen the last of me, though. There's no reason at all why I shouldn't drop in on my dear half-brother occasionally—and if you need me again, just say the word. It's given me one hell of a kick to let Jake think I was taking his wife to bed. He sure wasn't happy, I can tell you. We nearly came to blows more than once.'

'You didn't have to go on with it,' said Ivory.

'I'd have been a fool not to,' grinned Giles. 'It's the first time in my life that I've ever got Jake going. I reckon I should be thanking you for the pleasure.'

They held hands across the table and Ivory was almost tempted to tell him the real reason why she had left Jacob. Irresponsible Giles might be, but he had done her a big favour without ever demanding to know why she had asked. Not many people would have done that. He deserved more than the raw deal Jacob had handed him.

They chatted for over half an hour while Giles ate his sandwiches and informed her that he was returning to America the next day to join his parents and Valma.

'I'd rather you didn't tell her I'm back with Jacob,' said Ivory uneasily, feeling the other woman might come racing back to stake her claim.

'I won't even tell her I've seen you,' replied Giles with a reassuring grin, 'but I think she's got the message. She's taken a job in America. That can only mean she's given up on Jake.'

Ivory was feeling a whole lot better when she got back home. Giles, with his irrepressible carefree manner had done her good, and she felt ready to face as many of Jacob's business associates as he cared to bring.

She showered and dressed carefully, and when Jacob arrived was ready. If her smile was over-bright he did not notice, greeting her lovingly, introducing her with pride to his guests. No one would have believed that he did not love her.

'A new dress, darling?' he enquired, eyeing the gold silk which outlined the soft curves of her body. It concealed yet provoked and Ivory grew warm beneath his probing gaze. She felt sure he was seeing the woman who had given herself so freely to him last night, not the costly material which had eaten up her meagre savings.

She smiled briefly and nodded, and he turned to their visitors. 'Think yourselves lucky you're not married, gentlemen. Wives can be very expensive.'

Except that when money came as easily as it

did to him there was no need to count the cost, thought Ivory bitterly. What would he say now, she wondered, if she volunteered the information that she had bought this dress with her own money. It would not put him in a very good light, in fact it might ruin the whole evening.

But the men began talking and her opportunity was lost. Most of the time they discussed business, although Ivory was never left out of the conversation for long. They clearly envied Jacob his young and attractive wife and their open admiration was a splendid tonic for Ivory's morale.

She sailed through the evening as though she had been entertaining all her life, but it was not until towards the end, when Jacob was involved in a heated discussion with the oldest of the two men, that Ivory was shaken out of her calm.

She had been talking quietly to Michael, their other guest, trying to ignore the way his eyes kept sliding over her body, when suddenly he slipped a white card into her hand, glancing covertly at Jacob as he did so.

'I know Jacob's a busy man,' he said softly. 'You must spend a lot of evenings by yourself. If ever you feel like company give me a ring.'

Ivory stared for a few bemused seconds, colour flooding beneath her skin, before hissing savagely, 'How dare you! What sort of a girl do you take me for?'

Undaunted her companion grinned. 'I saw you with your—er, friend, at lunchtime. But don't worry, your secret's safe with me. I must admit I did not realise you were Jacob's wife at the time, I merely saw a very attractive woman.'

'My *friend*,' declared Ivory tightly, 'happened to be Jacob's half-brother, so please get your facts

right before insulting me with offers like that.'
She flung his card back at him, glaring angrily.

He looked embarrassed and put it into his
pocket. 'I'm sorry, Ivory. No hard feelings, I hope?'

'None at all,' she said with quiet dignity, but
found it very hard to be civil after that. Had he
really thought she was so free and easy with her
body? Thank goodness Jacob had not heard, or
he would probably have pulverised him.

But she was mistaken in thinking that her
husband had missed the conversation. As soon as
they were alone he turned on her, his face grim
and purposeful. 'Correct me if I'm wrong, but
did I hear you say you'd been out with Giles?'

Ivory flinched at the hardness in his tone. 'I
did see him, yes.'

'Despite my instructions that you were to keep
away?'

'It was purely accidental.' Her chin tilted
slightly, her brown eyes flashing. She was in no
mood to take chastisement from Jacob, especially
for something that had been completely innocent.

'It was enough to give Michael the wrong
impression,' he grated. 'It's not pleasant to have
my wife solicited by another man.'

'So you did hear?' Ivory's eyes flashed coldly.
'Why didn't you do something about it?'

'I was waiting to see how you handled him.'
His face was very hard, more angular than she
had ever remembered.

'To see whether I said yes?' she flung
incautiously. 'To see whether that's the type of
girl I've become?'

'I have my reasons,' he said coldly, 'and don't
fear, I shall be having a word with Michael—even
though it will probably mean I shall lose the
order.'

She eyed him narrowly. 'You surprise me. I thought making money came before everything else, even your wife's honour.'

His lips thinned. 'What is important to me is your relationship with Giles. I'm warning you now that if you dare to see him again I won't be responsible for my actions. You're mine, is that clear? No other man is to touch you.'

'You've left it a little late to say that.' Ivory wondered from where she found the nerve to stand up to him.

He frowned harshly. 'Did I have any choice? Wouldn't you have gone whether I forbade you or not?'

'Yes,' said Ivory clearly and was pleased when she saw the pain in his eyes. It was not very often she got the better of Jacob.

His lovemaking that night was tempered with anger. Nevertheless his savage movements incited in Ivory an excitement that she had not felt before and her response was more feverish than at any other time.

During the ensuing weeks Ivory's life followed a similar pattern. It was a routine she found boring. Jacob no longer pressed gifts or money on her so she could not even go out on a shopping spree. Buying the gold evening dress had reduced her bank balance to nil and because she was too proud to ask for money she filled in her time by altering her other dresses to fit.

He never asked what she had been doing and so long as she was there to entertain his guests, and keep him happy in bed, that was all he seemed to care.

It was not an ideal existence, but she supposed it was no more than she could expect, considering he had paid off her debts. Her aunt, now that she was no longer worried about Ivory, improved in health. Ivory telephoned her every day, but since she had no car of her own, and the journey was tedious by public transport, she did not visit her very often.

The strain began to show. Heavy shadows developed beneath her eyes and the weight continued to drop off her until even Jacob commented upon it.

Normally she was careful not to undress in front of him. She tried to keep herself to herself as much as possible, submitting reluctantly to his lovemaking because there was no other course open to her, usually ending up thoroughly enjoying the experience. It was one field in which they were entirely compatible.

One evening, however, Jacob came home early, surprising her as she walked naked from the shower into their room. His frown was harsh as he saw her prominent hip-bones, her ribs protruding through the translucent whiteness of her skin.

'My God!' he exclaimed loudly, harshly. 'You look like someone out of Belsen. What the hell have you been doing to yourself?'

Ivory snatched her silk robe and held it defiantly in front of her. 'Isn't it obvious?' She looked at him with cold dislike, struggling for the breath which had suddenly deserted her.

'It's insanity,' he declared angrily, plucking the garment from her nerveless fingers, fixing his steely blue eyes on the angular contours of her body. 'Why, Ivory? Why?'

'If you don't know the answer I'm not telling you,' she said tightly.

'You're not happy here? It's still Giles you love, is that it?' His lips were compressed so as to

be almost invisible, and there was a stillness
about him that was frightening.

'Since you ask . . .' Her voice was slightly
husky. 'No, I am not happy here. I imagined you
knew that. But I have no intention of backing out
of our bargain. I shall remain until you consider
my debt paid.' It was difficult to hold on to her
pride when she had no clothes to hide behind.

'At the expense of starving yourself to death?'
snorted Jacob savagely. 'What the hell do you
take me for, Ivory?'

'A sadist?' she enquired recklessly.

He growled and before she could move his long
lean fingers bit into her shoulders, the imprint of
each one of them making itself felt so that she
wanted to cry out with pain.

'If that's what you think,' he snarled, 'then
maybe I should behave like one. God, I was a
fool to ever let you go.'

'I was the fool for marrying you in the first
place,' she returned quietly. 'I should have
known there was no love in your heart.'

'You think that?' he attacked furiously.

'I know it.' Her chin tilted aggressively.
'You're too much a man of the world to fall for
someone like me.'

'Then why did I ask you to marry me?'

'For reasons of your own that you wouldn't
even tell me if I asked.'

'I see.' He was very still. 'And why did you
agree?'

'Because I was too naïve to know the difference
between love and physical attraction.'

He let her go suddenly and picking up the robe
he had discarded thrust it at her. While she
shrugged into it he turned away. 'At least we
both know where we stand. But don't think it will

make any difference. You are my wife and no man is ever going to take you from me again, ever.'

Ivory was not sure that she understood his reason since he had only married her to get his hands on his uncle's money. Unless, of course, it was his pride that had been hurt.

'How about Valma?' she enquired acidly. 'Where does she fit into all this? Or are you expecting me to share you with her? Is that to be my final humiliation?'

Jacob gave a snort of impatience. 'You're going out of your mind. Valma's gone. Get dressed. I'll take you out for a meal. I must have been blind not to see this happening.'

'I'm not hungry,' returned Ivory defensively.

His eyes had never been so coldly blue. 'Hungry or not, you're eating, even if I have to force it down your throat myself.' He went to her wardrobe and pulled out a cerise dress with an unusual appliqued leaf pattern over one shoulder. 'When I've had my shower I expect you to be ready.'

Ivory wondered whether she dared rebel. He looked in one hell of a mood, but who did he think he was, her keeper? He had no right speaking to her like this. Or did the fact that he'd paid off thirty-thousand pounds give him that right?

Reluctantly she dragged on the dress, tugging a brush through her hair so that it fell sleek and heavy about her shoulders. The deep pink suited her dark colouring, even though the material hung shapelessly over her thin body.

She applied more make-up than usual to hide the pallor in her cheeks and disguise the hollows beneath her eyes, and when Jacob came back into the room she was ready.

His glance held more than cursory interest. 'You look like nobody's child. Have you nothing that fits better than that?'

Ivory shrugged. 'Not really.'

'Then why don't you buy something?'

She eyed him belligerently. 'Because I have no money.'

He swore savagely. 'You could have asked.'

'I wouldn't ask you if I hadn't a rag to my back,' she said coldly, 'and the way things are at the moment I couldn't care less what I look like.' This was not strictly true, she liked to look her best at all times, but he was aggravating her to such an extent that she wanted to hit back.

'I care,' he snapped. 'I'm not having my wife look like an orphan. You can go shopping tomorrow and get yourself an entire new wardrobe.'

'And then when—if—I put weight back on—they'll be no good,' she exclaimed fiercely.

'As if I care!'

She had never seen him so infuriated by something that was really of no importance. 'That's right, throw your money away. Easy come, easy go, is that what they say?' Her eyes flashed angrily. 'If you'd had to work hard for your riches you wouldn't be so free.'

He looked at her coldly. 'And what is that supposed to mean?'

Ivory turned away. She had said too much already. 'Nothing. I was being stupid. Shall we go?'

To her relief he asked no further questions, leading the way from the apartment to his silver-grey Ferrari which roared into life like an angry monster at the turn of the key.

Cars were like people, thought Ivory, and

Jacob had chosen his well. He always drove fast sporty cars and this one had long sleek lines which housed a powerful engine, just as Jacob's lean hard body moulded a powerful physique.

He drove in silence, lips compressed, his long, always perfectly manicured, fingers holding the wheel loosely but competently.

It was the first time he had taken her out since she had come back to live with him, and in the close confines of his car Ivory could not escape the sexual magnetism that emanated from him.

She felt trapped, ensnared in a web of sensualism so thick it threatened to choke her. It was what had attracted her to him in the first place, a compelling force that could not be ignored, and even though she despised him for what he had done to her, there was no denying the chemistry that bonded them together.

He wore a light grey pin-striped suit, very correct and very business-like, yet it affected her possibly more than if he had worn tight jeans and an open shirt.

She swallowed and found her mouth dry, and wondered if he knew exactly what it was he did to her. In bed she could shut her eyes to Jacob, the man, and enjoy only the pleasures he incited in her. Now, there was no blinding her senses. He was here beside her, excitingly, sexily, male, and the fact that he was angry with her made no difference at all. In fact it added to her awareness of him, heightened her emotions, made her pulses race all out of time with themselves.

Expecting him to take her to one of the fashionable restaurants in the city itself, she was surprised when he nosed the car towards the country, stopping at a low timbered place she had never noticed before. Jacob, however, was greeted with a warmth that suggested he was a regular customer, making Ivory wonder whether this was a favourite haunt when entertaining Valma.

She was given a discreet smile by the head waiter. 'Your usual table, Mr Pendragon?' he enquired, leading the way towards the far corner of the room.

The table was set apart from the others, affording an intimacy that Ivory did not feel she could cope with.

Jacob shook his head. 'Not tonight, Henry. This one, I think.' He indicated a table in the centre, and although Ivory felt relieved she could not help wondering whether he had done it because he did not want her to take the place he normally associated with his silver-blonde girl-friend. If that was the case, why had he brought her here? Why not choose somewhere that held no memories at all?

She felt very bitter as she took her seat, eyeing him rebelliously when he enquired what she would like to drink. 'Something strong,' she grated through her teeth. If she was to get through the evening she would need her spirits bolstering.

He raised an eyebrow and ordered her a gin and tonic, waiting until the waiter was out of earshot before saying, 'I hope it is not your intention to get drunk. I have no intention of taking an inebriate wife to bed with me tonight.'

She looked at him coldly. 'Do you bring Valma here?'

'I have done,' he admitted carelessly. 'But I can't see that it's of any consequence.'

'To me it is,' she hissed. 'I don't like being looked at as though I'm another of your fancy women. You could have chosen somewhere different.'

To her annoyance he looked amused. 'I happen to like it here, and I can assure you Henry thought no such thing.'

'How do you know what he's thinking?' she cried irrationally.

'I've known Henry a long time. But I have no intention of sitting here all night discussing the virtues of Henry. I've brought you here because the food is excellent and I intend seeing that you eat everything that is put on your plate.'

About to declare vehemently that she was not a child, that she would eat what she wanted and to hell with him, she decided that arguing was childish too. She clamped her lips and stared at him mutinously.

His slow smile increased her anger and when her gin was placed in front of her she downed it in one swallow and asked for another. But Jacob shook his head. 'It's not wise on an empty stomach, my darling.'

Ivory bristled angrily. 'Don't darling me, I'm in no mood for it.'

He sipped his whisky, surveying her calmly over the rim of his glass. 'Going out for a meal with your husband should be a pleasurable occasion. Let's make it one.'

'Why?' Her lids snapped haughtily. 'I'm living with you under sufferance. I'm here because you forced me. But there's no way you can make me enjoy it.'

'That's a pity,' he said quietly, and he sounded as though he genuinely regretted the fact. 'I'd hoped that once Giles was out of your hair you'd realise exactly what it was you had given up. We were happy once, I'm quite sure.'

'There's only one thing you're good at,' she said pointedly, 'and I can do without that.'

His eyes hardened and she saw the tensing of his jaw. 'Is that so? I hardly think you'd find life bearable without the—pleasure of making love.' He waved away the waiter who hovered with the menus. 'It is the only thing that is keeping you sane, if I read you correctly.'

'Try me,' she ground out bitterly.

'I intend to,' came the surprising reply. 'In future, dear wife, I shall not lay one finger on you. If you want me, you will be the one who does the asking.'

'In that case, we may as well go our separate ways.' Brown eyes held blue in silent hostility.

The smile that curved his lips held menace, not pleasure. 'Oh, no, that would be far too easy. We shall continue to live together and still sleep together.'

'Then you'll be punishing yourself, not me,' she cried savagely, blinking back the sting of tears that threatened to ruin her composure.

'We shall see. I pride myself on being able to control my—er, feelings, a little better than you. Shall we order?'

Ivory had not been hungry before they came out, now the thought of food choked her. Nevertheless she made a brave effort to eat all that was placed before her, watched by the unnerving eye of Jacob.

Little was said until they reached the coffee stage and Ivory asked for a brandy to go with it.

'Since you've already drunk more than half a bottle of wine,' said Jacob, 'I think not. Or is it still your intention to drink yourself senseless? Perhaps you now have a reason for doing so?'

Ivory felt like hitting him over the head with

the bottle, only the fact that the restaurant was full making her hang on to her temper.

A satisfied glitter appeared in Jacob's blue eyes as she curled her fingers into her palms, visibly restraining herself. 'Perhaps a small one, and then I'll take you home before you pass out.'

Ivory hated to admit that he was right, that the wine had gone to her head, and her reason for drinking so much was because she was afraid of sleeping with him. It would be agony sharing the same bed, knowing that he was not going to lay one finger on her.

'I think,' he said, 'that it would be a good idea if you had a holiday. We'll go down to Cornwall. The fresh air should give you an appetite—and it's about time I took a break myself.'

Ivory eyed him stubbornly. 'I don't like Cornwall,' she said. 'At least I don't like your house.' It held nothing but unhappy memories. It was there that she had discovered the true reason Jacob had married her. She hated the place.

'You have no say in the matter. We'll leave tomorrow afternoon. I shall need to go into the office in the morning to sort things out. I'll drop you off to do your shopping, and we'll go after lunch.'

There was no point in arguing. There never was any point in arguing with Jacob. Only once had she opposed him, and look where that had got her.

She shrugged and drank her coffee and brandy. Shortly after that they were on their way home.

The alcohol did its job. No sooner did her head hit the pillow than she was asleep. The next thing she knew Jacob was roughly shaking her. 'Come on, Ivory, I have to leave in half an hour. We're going to Blackstone today, don't forget.' His mouth twisted wryly. 'A second honeymoon—if you care to make it that way.'

CHAPTER SEVEN

THE journey down to Cornwall reminded Ivory
of that first time he had taken her to his family
home. Her first sight of the house had been a
disappointment. She had felt its brooding
atmosphere and had been convinced she would
not be happy there.

How right she had been. Not many wives, she
guessed, left their husbands on their honeymoon.
Neither, she thought wryly, did they have their
husband's former lovers joining them. It had
been Valma's intrusion that had done it, Valma's
gleeful citation that Jacob had married her merely
to get his hands on his uncle's money.

It was a bombshell that could not be ignored.
It had made her see Jacob in a new light,
understand why he had married her when there
was such a vast difference in their ages and
lifestyle.

And now he was taking her there again! She
needed a holiday, he said, but what peace would
she get there? At least she would be thankful that
Valma was in America. There could be no one to
intrude on their privacy. Not that she had any
wish to be alone with Jacob. His reason for
joining her was a mystery. It would have made
more sense had he shipped her off alone.

Unless it was to torment her with his presence?
He had sworn never to touch her again unless she
did the asking. And he knew how she reacted to
his nearness. It was a physical thing that she
would never be able to ignore.

The journey seemed endless, but she refused to speak, not once answering his attempts at conversation. What point was there? she thought tiredly. The whole exercise was a waste of time, doomed to failure before it had begun. She wanted nothing more to do with Jacob, he was taking advantage of her yet again. He had no interest in her as a person, as a wife, he was punishing her for walking out on him on their honeymoon.

When she had got into financial difficulties he had seen this as a way of getting back at her. He did not really care that she was losing weight, he could not do. He did not really care what she looked like, unless it was to save his own face. It would not look good when entertaining his colleagues if his wife was a walking skeleton. They would wonder what he was doing to her—and that would not do at all.

When she consistently refused to speak he clamped his lips and drove faster than she had ever known before. There was a recklessness about him which aroused in her a bitter anger. Jacob was so used to getting his own way that when anyone opposed him he could not handle it.

Ivory concentrated her attention on the passing scenery. Spring was one of the most beautiful seasons of the year. The fresh colour of the leaves, lambs gambolling in the fields, it was all so breathtaking.

But as they drew nearer to Jacob's home, as they turned off the main road at Jamaica Inn she felt a tightening of her stomach muscles. Blackstone. A house of unhappiness. How was she going to cope with living here with Jacob for however long it took his fancy?

She glanced across and was pleased to see that

his face was as grim as her own thoughts. His lips were compressed, his square chin taut, skin drawn tightly across angular cheek-bones, and the hands that gripped the wheel were white at the knuckles. A sure sign that he was having difficulty in controlling his feelings. In fact she could never remember seeing him so wound up. It did not bode well for the time they were about to spend together.

The track down to the house had not improved. In fact it was even more rutted and pot-holed than before. She expected Jacob to slow down but he made no attempt to reduce his speed and they bounced over the uneven surface until Ivory felt as though her inside was jolting out.

But she said nothing. What point was there? Jacob was furious with her for ignoring him on the journey down. If she dared ask him to take it easy now he would tell her, in no uncertain words, to mind her own business.

She clung on to the edge of her seat, holding her lips as firm as his. Not until they rounded the final bend and she saw the windows of Blackstone sparkle a welcome in the sunshine did she let out an involuntary gasp.

The flower-beds surrounding the big stone house were neat and tidy, full of spring flowers nodding their heads in the slight breeze that swept across the countryside. The lawns were green and trim. Before it had looked neglected. Now it looked like home, and she glanced across at Jacob, but her unspoken question went unanswered.

Without even looking at her he turned off the engine and climbed quickly from the car. He took their cases from the boot and unlocking the front door strode inside and straight upstairs.

Ivory followed at a more leisurely pace, taking in the pristine freshness of the place, the immaculate paintwork, crisp curtains. Instead of going upstairs she pushed open the door to the sitting room. Some of the old furniture had gone, some still remained, polished to a lustre that pleased the eye.

It was neat and clean and she hated to say this, but welcoming! A fire was laid in the hearth waiting for the touch of a match to burst into flame, to warm the room and its occupants. Unable to believe that such a change had been wrought Ivory went through into the kitchen.

This time she could not control a gasp of surprise. It had been completely remodelled. Solid oak units lined the walls, a sparkling stainless-steel sink stood beneath the crystal clear windows. A new freezer, a split level cooker. In fact every modern convenience a woman could want.

Completely bemused by now she turned and followed Jacob's path up the stairs. The door to their bedroom stood open. She could not believe that it was the same room. The old dark furniture had disappeared, replaced by modern units with clean pleasing lines. A deep-piled carpet covered the boarded floor, an oyster silk spread embroidered with pink roses lay across the bed. It was feminine, yet not too much so, and it pleased her far more than she cared to admit.

Jacob stood near the window. 'What's happened?' she whispered hesitantly. 'Why the change? Who's been living here?'

'No one.' He sounded bitter. 'But I'm glad you like it. I left instructions that it was to be given a face-lift. I hadn't realised until you came here how gloomy it was. It suited me. I came down for

peace and quiet. I was blind to my surroundings.
It did not matter whether I lived in a cave or a
palace. You opened my eyes.'

She looked at him sharply, but there was no
emotion on his face. He was not even looking at
her. He could have been speaking to himself.
'When was it done?'

'Not long after you left,' he admitted. 'I
thought you'd come back. I never realised your
infatuation for Giles would last as long as it did.
It was stupid of me, I suppose. What do you
think of it?'

Ivory shook her head. He was asking her this
question but it did not sound as though he really
cared. She shrugged. 'It's all right. It's an
improvement at least. But Blackstone is
Blackstone. It always will be. The house has a
feel about it. No matter what you do it won't
change that.'

He sighed and snapped open her suitcase,
suggesting she unpack and then join him
downstairs for a meal. He had looked oddly
disappointed by her reaction, which surprised
Ivory. Why should it affect him?

Left on her own Ivory wandered over to the
window, looking out at the tor which rose high
above the house, at the granite boulders strewing
its slopes, yellow gorse, a lark circling overhead.
At the blue, blue sky marred only by a few fluffy
white clouds.

She really ought to be at peace here. It was not
the most beautiful place in the world, but it was a
spot that could, she supposed, get through to you
if you let it.

The very barrenness of the moor had a strange
appeal that perhaps only a few ever felt. Jacob felt
it. But then Jacob had been born here. It was in

his blood. It was a part of him. Despite his
success he was a man who liked to be alone to
enjoy the wide open spaces. Somehow Ivory felt
she would never be able to come to terms with it,
or him!

Eventually she hung away her clothes in the
wardrobes, folded jumpers and undies into the
drawers with their lining of lavender-scented
paper. Whoever had done the work for Jacob had
given thought to every tiny detail, even down to a
bowl of flowers on the dresser.

When it was all done she still felt reluctant to
go downstairs. Instead she went along to the
bathroom. Here again the old suite had been
ripped out. A brand new bath in a warm mink
colour took its place, a shower cubicle, a
washbasin and bidet, all complete with gold
fittings.

No expense had been spared and she wondered
why it had taken her argument with him to
persuade him to remodernise the house. It was
certainly an improvement. She ought to love it
but she refused to believe that it had been done
for her benefit. More than likely it was because of
Valma. He had probably spent a considerable
amount of his time down here with her. If her
parents lived in Bodmin it was pretty obvious
that whenever he was in residence here she would
join him.

Her stomach knotted again with that familiar
tightness. She doubted she would ever be able to
get Valma out of her system. Not that it
mattered. Their marriage was over, finished. It
had been a non-starter from the beginning.

She had just emerged from the shower, a soft
brown towel draped about her, when Jacob came
up the stairs. 'You've taken your time,' he said,

but although his voice was angry his eyes took in
the long length of her thighs, the creamy skin of
her painfully thin shoulders.

Before she had time to realise his intentions he
ripped the towel away, looking at her body with a
light in his eyes that Ivory for once could not
understand.

It was not lust, nor desire, more a clinical
analysis. She felt utterly defenceless but refused
to give him the satisfaction of covering herself
with her hands. Instead she eyed him belligerently, quivering when he reached out and
touched her, stroking her tiny breasts, lingering
on the hollow of her waist, resting on jutting hip
bones, sliding down her thighs, before turning
away with a gesture of disgust.

For a brief second she saw pain in his eyes and
wondered whether it was self-deprecation,
whether he knew he had done this to her. She
snorted silently. It was hardly likely. If the truth
was known he couldn't give a damn. She felt
somehow soiled where his fingers had touched
her and cringed backwards, tempted to take
another shower.

His eyes narrowed and she felt he was going to
lunge out, then he turned abruptly and went back
down the stairs. She moved into their bedroom
and slowly pulled on one of the new dresses she
had bought that morning.

It was turquoise silk emblazoned with scarlet
poppies. It made her look even skinnier, she
decided, looking at herself in the full-length mirror
on the wardrobe door. She had had no interest in
what she bought, merely picking up one dress after
another, adding them to her pile of purchases.

If Jacob thought that bringing her down here
was going to make her indulge in an orgy of

eating he was mistaken. The very thought of food
nauseated her, Jacob's presence neauseated her.
She wished she had never set eyes on him.

In the breakfast room she discovered that a
meal was waiting. A steak and kidney pie sat in
the centre of the table, steam rising from the slits
in the top. It looked golden and delicious. On
either side were bowls of vegetables and she
looked at him questioningly.

'I have a new housekeeper,' he said. 'She's a
superb cook as you can see. She has agreed to
come in each day to cook our meals.'

Ivory flicked him a cold look. 'Are you
suggesting that I cannot cope?'

'I am suggesting you might not have the
inclination,' he said impatiently. 'It is my
intention to take you out in the fresh air, to bring
you back here so hungry that you'll do justice to
the meals Mrs Trevelyan cooks, and sleep as
soundly as a new-born babe. In no time at all, I
hope, you'll be back to your former self.'

'And what then?' snapped Ivory. 'Back to the
grindstone in London? Is your wife no longer
attractive enough to be your hostess, is that it? Is
that why you've brought me here? Are you
ashamed of me?'

Jacob looked as though he would like to hit
her. Instead he sat down and began heaping
potatoes and carrots and a portion of pie on to
both of their plates.

Ivory turned her back and walked out, but she
had gone no more than a couple of steps when he
was behind her, his hand on her arm, pulling her
roughly, savagely backwards, forcing her into the
chair. 'Eat, damn you!' he ground. 'Eat, or I'll
ram it down your throat myself. And I mean that.
The way you're going you'll kill yourself.'

'As if I care,' cried Ivory heatedly.

'You think I don't?' There was a pained expression on his face.

She looked at him coldly, refusing to believe what she saw. 'I know you don't. If you cared about me you'd never have let me go. You used me, Jacob, and I hate you. Do you know that? With every fibre of my being I hate you, and if starving myself to death is the only way I can get away from you, then that is what I will do.'

She trembled from head to toe, and disgust rose in her throat threatening to suffocate her.

'You little fool,' he snarled, his lips firming into that thin line she knew so well. 'I won't pretend to understand what you mean, but running away solves nothing. It might interest you to know that letting you go was the worst thing I ever did. I should have forced you to stay.'

'A lot of good that would have done,' she cried, the cold blue of his eyes frightening her. Maybe she was mistaken antagonising Jacob. They were alone in this place. He could do anything. Anything! But even so she carried on. 'You'd have made me hate you even more than I do at this moment. You have no right doing this to me, Jacob. I didn't want to come here and you're not going to make me eat. To hell with your food.' She picked up the plate and flung it at him.

He ducked instinctively and it smashed against the window, shattering the glass, showering mashed potato and gravy everywhere.

Appalled by what she had done, but unwilling to apologise, Ivory got up and ran. She was not sure whether she expected Jacob to follow, but he didn't.

She walked for miles, or what seemed like

miles, before finally flinging herself down on the short springy turf, burying her head in her hands, and crying until there were no tears left.

Yet even then she did not feel better. She felt a burning rage inside her, resentment that Jacob should dare to do this to her, dare to ask that she go on living as his wife, force her to come here, when he had no more interest in her than—that fly walking on her hand.

She dashed it away impatiently. Damn Jacob! Damn Blackstone! Damn everything!

She got up and began walking again, further and further away from the house, forcing herself to move until her legs would carry her no longer. Then she sank down and rested her head against a hillock of grass, watching the sun set, the sky burst into flame, shivering as it began to grow cold. Finally becoming afraid as darkness settled over the moor.

She had never been out here by herself at night. All sorts of alien sounds and cries reached her ears. The high-pitched screech of an owl, the shuffle of an animal as it made its way through the undergrowth.

She wanted to go back, but was unsure which frightened her most, the darkness out here, or Jacob. She did not want to spend the night with Jacob. She could not bear the thought of lying in bed beside him, her body aching for his touch while he let her suffer.

It was easy to imagine him gloating over his victory. She wished it was summer and warm enough to sleep beneath the stars. In spring the night air was cold and she began to shiver, her teeth chattering so much that she knew it was stupidity to stay out any longer.

Her feet dragged as she slowly made her way

back towards Blackstone. As she topped the tor
and looked down at the house every window
blazed, even the door stood open, yellow light
spilling out on to the path.

It was like a tiny doll's house from up here, yet
surprisingly looked warm and friendly, unlike her
memories of the place. There was a homeliness
about it that beckoned her and she found herself
hurrying, her footsteps faltering only when she
saw Jacob standing in the doorway.

She came to a full-stop in front of him. He
made no move to stand back and let her in. For
several long minutes they stood there, weighing
each other up. 'I was just about to come after
you,' said Jacob at length.

'You expect me to believe that?' she scoffed. 'I
doubt you even thought about me.'

He looked at her coldly. 'I thought about you
all right. It was quite a mess you made. I hope
you felt good.'

'Very good,' she returned, 'and if you're
expecting me to apologise, forget it. I'd do the
same again. Let me in, please, I'm going to bed.'

'Not until you've eaten.' He spoke slowly,
menacingly, his eyes watchful.

'I'm not hungry,' returned Ivory defensively.

'I couldn't give a damn whether you're
hungry or not,' Jacob breathed harshly, 'but
you're going to eat.' His long powerful fingers
clamped her wrist and she cried out in hurt
outrage as he dragged her mercilessly into the
kitchen.

A saucepan of soup simmered on the hotplate.
He sat her at the brand new breakfast bar and
poured the soup into a waiting pot-bellied mug,
placing it silently in front of her.

When she made no attempt to touch it he said

firmly, 'Drink, Ivory. I want no more histrionics.'
There was something about him that told her it
would be fatal to refuse, a grimness, an air of
impatience, determination. He looked, she
thought, like a man reaching the end of his tether,
and she felt a grim satisfaction that she was able
to do this to him.

Nevertheless she obediently took a sip of the
soup. It was surprisingly good, although she had
no doubt that it had come out of a tin. She
wrapped her fingers about the mug, allowing the
warmth to seep into her bones, taking another
sip, and another, feeling it nourish her.

Not until she had finished every drop did
Jacob move. It seemed that he gave a sigh of
relief, yet no sound escaped his lips. He looked
hurt, which surprised her. Jacob was usually top
dog, no one hurt him. He was the one who
handed out punishment.

He took the mug and rinsed it beneath the tap,
apparently surprised to find her still sitting there
when he turned around. 'You can go to bed now,'
he said. 'I'll be up shortly.'

Ivory's eyelids flickered uncertainly, having
Jacob in bed beside her was the last thing she
wanted. But she knew there was no point in
arguing, just as there had been no point in
refusing to drink the soup. Perhaps, with a bit of
luck, she might be asleep before he came, and
then he would be unable to rejoice in the agony
which lying beside him would cause her.

Not surprisingly, though, sleep evaded her.
She listened to him moving downstairs, growing
more tense with every minute, aware that all too
soon his footsteps would sound on the stairs.

When eventually she heard him coming she
went rigid. Her heart missed a beat. She turned

on her side and drew her knees up to her chin,
hoping he would believe she was asleep.

She heard the rustle of his shirt against his skin
as he stripped it from his powerful chest. She
heard the zip of his trousers and the movement as
he slid them from his legs. But not until he left
the room to take his shower did she realise she
had been holding her breath.

Taking in a deep gulp of air she sat up, her
eyes wide, listening to the jet stream of water,
imagining it caressing his body. It was her hands
that should be touching him. She loved him. No
matter how often, or how violently she told
herself that she hated him, she did not. She
would love him for all time—regardless how
cruelly he treated her, despite what he said or
what he did. It was a fact of life. An indisputable
fact. There was nothing at all that she could do
about it.

When she finally heard the shower being
turned off she slid down again beneath the sheets,
pulling them about her face, hoping she could
hide herself from him.

She heard him towelling his hair, the vigorous
rub with which she was all too familiar. Normally
she watched him dry himself, loving every
intimate detail about him.

His hand was less than gentle when he
snatched back the sheets and lowered himself in
bed beside her. He smelt of musk and the warm
dampness of his body was as evocatively sensual
as she had known it would be.

He made no attempt to keep to his side of the
bed. Although he had not spoken she guessed he
knew she was awake, that he was deliberately
lying close, hoping she would give in to the
longings, the cravings, that clamoured inside her.

Unlike last night she had no alcohol to dull her senses, to whisk her to sleep the moment her head touched the pillow. She was condemned to a night of heartache, and had no idea how she was going to get through it.

When Jacob's breathing told her that he was asleep she felt angry. How could he do this to her? How could he be so immune? It proved there was no emotion involved, that each time they made love it was from pure physical need and not because he loved her. He had never loved her. He was a greedy avaricious man who put money above all else.

Giles had lost out because of this. She herself, in the beginning, had gained. She had been showered with presents, with unwanted gifts, had felt flattered and loved. She had never known a man so generous.

What a stupid, blind fool she had been, how gullible, how innocent. In one way she had Valma to thank for opening her eyes. If Valma had not put her in the picture she would not have found out until it was too late, until Jacob had decided she could no longer be of any use to him. Probably not until he had spent all the money he had inherited.

The more she thought about the way he had treated her the more tense she became, until finally she crawled out of bed. Pulling her robe about her trembling limbs she made her way downstairs in search of the drinks cupboard.

Before the house had been done up it was always kept in the sitting room, but now the cabinet had disappeared. She could not find a bottle anywhere. She began to feel quite desperate. Drinking herself silly was the only way she was going to get any sleep.

She searched feverishly, crying out in alarm
when she swung round and found Jacob watching
her. He had not bothered to put on any clothes
and stood there, his proud masculinity flaunted
for her to see.

'Damn you!' she cried.

'If it's a drink you're after you're doomed to
disappointment.' His voice was level, amused
even.

Ivory had expected him to be angry and was
surprised to see how calm he looked.

'How long have you been an alcoholic?' he
enquired coolly.

'I'm not,' she snapped. 'I don't touch the stuff
usually.'

His lips curled up at the corners. 'But—like
last night—you need something to help you sleep.
Is that it? You could always use me. It's the best
knock-out there is, believe me. It never fails to
work. You only have to ask.'

'Go to hell!' Incensed by his mockery Ivory
tried to push her way past him, but he caught her
in an iron-like grip that she felt sure must break
her bones.

Many times before she had felt defenceless in
front of him, but never as much as she did at this
moment. It was an experience that she had never
expected to encounter. The sheer aggressive
masculinity of his body reached out to her,
quickening her pulses, making her heart race,
until she felt like tearing off her nightdress and
begging him to make love.

Only pride made her tilt her chin. 'Let me go,
Jacob.' Her lashes hid her eyes and there was a
quiver to her voice. She despised herself for
allowing him to see that she was not totally
immune.

'Why should I?' Again that amused glitter to his eyes. 'You want me, why not admit it? Why not swallow that stubborn pride of yours then perhaps we might both get some sleep?'

'Never,' she cried desperately. 'Never, Jacob.'

He frowned harshly and pulled her hard against him. Ivory felt an instantaneous vibrating response and it took every ounce of will-power to remain unresponsive in his arms. She met his eyes coldly, stubbornly, refusing to acknowledge the clamouring of her senses.

After what seemed like minutes, but must have been seconds, he flung her from him with an angry gesture. Ivory raced back upstairs and after only a second's hesitation climbed into bed. She had a feeling that Jacob would not join her again that night.

Eventually she slept, not waking until the sunlight flickered across her face. Lethargically she opened her eyes, feeling warm and comfortable. Forgetting all that had gone on before she reached out and felt Jacob in bed beside her. Not until she was about to snuggle up to him did she remember the circumstances.

She shrank away and wondered how long he had been there. He was fast asleep. She leaned up on one elbow and looked down. His ridiculously long lashes fanned his cheeks, there was a slight smile on his lips and a flush to his skin. His hair was tousled and she had an insane urge to run her fingers through it.

Unable to help herself Ivory reached out and traced the long line of his jaw, feeling the stubble of hair, shrinking back only when his eyes shot open. He gave a lazy smile, stretching out his arms and pulling her over on top of him.

She began to struggle. 'Isn't this what you

were after?' he chuckled sensually. 'Isn't this what you have wanted all night?'

'No!' she cried. 'Never, never! For God's sake, Jacob, let me go. You can't do this to me, I won't let you. I hate you touching me. You repulse me.'

His face changed dramatically, a harsh frown creasing his brow, a glacial hardness to his eyes. Pushing her from him he flung out of bed and marched from the room.

Ivory felt deflated, as though she had been run over by a steamroller and left for dead. He had crushed her with one stinging glance. She guessed it would be a long time before he attempted to touch her again. Maybe never!

It should have made her feel good, but it didn't. She wanted to run after him, to tell him that she had not meant it, that she did not care if he married her for all the wrong reasons. She loved him, didn't he know that?

When he returned after his shower he said briskly, 'Get ready, Ivory, we're going into Padstow. It's May Day and they celebrate in a big way there. You'll enjoy it.'

'Who's saying I want to?' she enquired incautiously, still smarting over his rejection.

'I am,' he said firmly. 'You have no choice.'

Padstow was a quaint little town nestling below the cliffs, the houses built into the hillside, getting closer and closer together until they were huddled around the harbour.

Long before they reached the centre Jacob was compelled to park his car. They joined the jostling crowds and made their way towards the harbour.

It was a gloriously sunny day without a cloud in the sky. The streets were strung with flags, lamp-posts and doorways decked with sycamore branches, and there was an air of excitement and festivity that was contagious. They found themselves pushed along by the crowd to the Institute where, apparently, at ten the Blue Ribbon Oss would appear.

Already the master of ceremonies was strutting about in his top hat and tails. Men with drums, tambourines or accordians were poised in readiness, dressed in white trousers and shirts, with blue sashes or belts, and with white sailor caps trimmed with flowers.

Another man brandished a fancy club. 'That's the Teaser,' informed Jacob. Ivory was not altogether sure what he meant but decided to wait and find out rather than ask. Although the atmosphere was such that she had begun to relax there was still a long way to go before she would feel at ease with Jacob.

At ten on the dot the Blue Ribbon Oss made its spectacular appearance, its great hooped skirt lashing out at unsuspecting bystanders as he whirled and reared.

It was a very impressive sight. The man who carried the horse wore a grotesque black mask, decorated with coloured stripes, and a tall hat topped with a flowing horsehair plume tied with a blue ribbon.

His wooden snappers were also trimmed with horsehair, the jaws studded so that they made a loud noise when operated with strings by the man inside the voluminous skirt.

The accordians and drums burst forth with sound, singing broke out, and the horse pranced and was 'teased' by the Teaser with his club. It was as though he was being baited and Ivory now understood how the man got his name.

Then silence! The horse sank down. The

Teaser rested his club on the sailcloth skirt. A
slow song began. And then, just as suddenly, the
drums beat and the Oss came back to life.

Ivory was very impressed by all that was going
on, allowing the crowds to move her along as they
followed the Oss, not really very concerned when
she discovered she had become parted from
Jacob.

At eleven a similar ritual followed when the
Old Oss emerged from the Golden Lion Inn.
Their party of musicians wore red and white
spotted neckerchiefs as opposed to the blue of
their rivals.

For a time she followed the dancing and
singing procession through the streets. It amused
her to note that the paths of the horses never
crossed.

Suddenly Ivory found herself trapped beneath
the hooped skirt of the Blue Ribbon Oss. She had
seen it happen to others, some girls even offering
themselves to be caught, but she had not
expected it to happen to herself.

It was hot beneath the canvas and Ivory pitied
the poor man who had to carry this weight on his
shoulders for so long. Then she was free. Only to
be caught again by a strong pair of arms, pulled
backwards against a rock-hard body.

'You do realise what getting yourself trapped
by the Oss means?'

She twisted her head sharply at the sensuous
chuckle in her ear, looking up into Jacob's
laughing blue eyes. He seemed to be in an
extraordinary good humour all of a sudden.

The vibrant beat of his heart drummed against
her back, while the whipcord arms tightened
about her waist, and her legs were too close for
comfort to his muscular thighs. He awoke every

nerve in her body. She was so vitally aware of him that for the moment the milling crowds were forgotten.

She licked her suddenly dry lips. 'Wasn't it simply a bit of fun?'

'Oh, no!' He smiled wickedly and surprisingly pressed his lips into her hair.

It was impossible to escape and truthfully she did not want to. Everyone here today was letting down their hair. Laughing, singing, having fun. She felt as lighthearted and carefree as the rest and impulsively returned his smile, flirting with her eyes. If this was the way he wanted to play it, then so be it. 'You'd better put me out of my misery. Is the world going to fall about my head?'

He laughed and the sound warmed her, then he spun her round to face him. 'Nothing so dramatic. The horse is a fertility symbol, did you not know? According to tradition every woman caught beneath its skirt becomes either lucky or pregnant.'

Ivory giggled, she could not help herself. 'Don't tell me you believe that rubbish?' Not Jacob. Jacob was far too matter of fact. He never lived with his head in the clouds.

'I do,' he said, suddenly serious. 'And in your case I reckon you'll get a double-dose. First you'll realise exactly how much you love me, that's the lucky part, for me at least, and secondly I happen to think we should start a family straight away. It should prevent you running away a second time.'

Ivory's brown eyes were wider than they had ever been. He looked as though he meant every word. But wasn't today a time for revelry, for jokes and laughter? 'Very funny,' she said, and tried to laugh, but found she couldn't. Jacob *was* serious. It was there on his face, not the hint of a twinkle in those thickly framed eyes, not the ghost of a smile on his lips. 'You mean it?' she whispered. 'You're not joking?'

'I've never been more serious in my life.' He pressed his lips to her throat. 'I'm not going to let you go away again, Ivory. You've had your fun, but you're my wife, and you're going to stay that way for the rest of your life.'

CHAPTER EIGHT

IT was important, Ivory decided, to try and keep everything lighthearted. Jacob meant what he said, there was no doubt about that, but there was no way she could go on living with a man who did not love her.

For the moment though, she decided to humour him. She smiled into his face, trying unsuccessfully to ignore the way her pulses raced when she found his eyes resting disturbingly on her. He made no attempt to hide the fact that he desired her, and trying to stop herself from pressing even closer was virtually impossible.

Her body responded alarmingly to his, as though it felt that this was its rightful place, no matter what her mind dictated. His very masculinity threatened to consume her and there was a break in her voice as she spoke. 'It's the first time I've been here on May Day. Let's not miss it. Let's go and join the crowds.'

'To hell with them,' he said thickly. 'I want you, Ivory, you're driving me insane, do you know that, with your hands-off-me routine. Let's go home and make love. Don't deny me what I know you want as well.'

'I do want you, Jacob,' she admitted, burying her head against his chest, then wishing she hadn't because the clean male smell of him intoxicated her. 'But you know it doesn't mean a thing. It's pure body chemistry. Let's enjoy today. Let's just be friends. I want to join in the fun.'

'Are you suggesting that I ignore what you're doing to me? That I spend the day making polite conversation as though you mean no more to me than any girl I could have rescued from the horse?'

He sounded agonised and Ivory looked at him sharply. 'That's what I do mean, Jacob.' He would never know how much it cost her to say that. Seeing his anguished expression, adding it to her own inexplicable need of him, it would be so easy to give in. It was madness wanting Jacob like this. She ought to be ashamed of herself. There was more to life than sex for the sake of sex. Admittedly Jacob was the only man who could satisfy her in this way, but all he was doing was using her. He desired her, that was why he wanted her to go back to Blackstone now. Love did not enter into it.

'You drive a hard bargain, Ivory,' he said, his hands moving disquietingly over her back, moulding her against the long length of his hard masculine body.

She could not ignore his pulsating desire and her own breath came in quick short gasps. 'It has to be this way, Jacob, for both our sakes.'

'Why, in hell's name?' he rasped, cupping her face suddenly between lean bony fingers, clamping his mouth on hers. 'Why, Ivory?' he breathed harshly against her lips. 'Why deny us both the pleasure of satisfying our very natural urges?'

Why indeed, when she wanted it as much as he? When her heart raced fit to burst, pounding painfully against her ribcage, throbbing against the solid wall of his chest.

'Because,' she whispered tremulously, 'that is the way it has to be. I don't want to get hurt again.'

'Again?' he pounced, frowning harshly. 'Have I ever hurt you? It strikes me that you were the one who did the hurting, leaving me for Giles like you did. You've no idea how much it cost to let you go.'

But you did, she cried inside. You could have begged me to stay, you could have professed undying love. But no, you were glad to get rid of me. Aloud she said, 'Don't lie to me, Jacob. If the truth's known you were relieved.'

'How can you say that?' He held her head tightly, covering her face with urgent kisses. His breath was warm on her cheek, his lips fevered as they scorched every inch of her face. 'I need you, Ivory, God how I need you.'

It was not the first time she had heard these words. It would be a very hard woman who could ignore his plea. But Ivory had learned to be hard. 'If you need a woman that badly . . .' She managed to inject a note of acidity into her voice, 'it shouldn't be too difficult to find one. There were plenty offering themselves to be trapped by the Osses. Maybe they're ready for a cheap thrill, I'm not. I meant it when I said I did not want you to make love to me again. I'm prepared to spend the day with you, but on my terms, not yours.'

As she spoke his face hardened and by the time she had finished he had put her from him. They were alone for the moment, the crowds having followed the two horses on their lively journey through the streets.

Ivory could hear the sound of laughter and music but there was no joy in the hearts of either herself or Jacob. In fact he looked positively evil.

'How can you say that, Ivory? You know it's you I want. It has been from the first day I saw you. The rest of the world can go to hell for all I care.'

'I'm sorry, Jacob,' she said quietly, 'but I don't believe you. I know why you married me, and it certainly wasn't because I was the most irresistible woman in the world.'

His blue eyes pierced her and she was unable to look away. 'So far as I am concerned, there is only one reason why a man asks a woman to marry him. Are you suggesting that I had different ideas?'

'There *should* be only one reason,' said Ivory quietly, 'but with men like you love is the last thing on their mind.'

He gripped the soft flesh of her forearms and shook her violently. 'Men like me? What is it you're trying to say?'

He was coldly angry and she moistened her dry lips. 'I really can't see the point in discussing this. Once I've paid my debt to you I shall go. You'll never see me again, Jacob. There's simply no point in us remaining together.'

'You're talking in riddles,' he snapped harshly. 'I haven't the slightest idea what you're on about, but I mean to get to the bottom of it, make no mistake. Our marriage will work, I promise you that.' He fixed his mouth on hers, his hands moving to cradle her head so that she found it impossible to escape.

While his lips were on hers she could believe him. Joined together like this it was easy to forget that Jacob had used her. She wanted to submit to his embrace, announce herself ready to take him on again. Only a very tiny part of her mind issued warning messages. But they were sufficiently urgent for her to heed them. She moved her head in a desperate effort to be free. 'No, Jacob, I won't. *I won't.* I'm sorry, but that's the way it must be.'

He continued to kiss her as though she had not spoken, his hand moving to the small of her back, pulling her inexorably against him. His whole body throbbed with a fierceness which matched her own.

Glancing over his shoulder Ivory saw an old woman watching from an upstairs window, and she increased her struggles, not liking the idea of a witness to their emotional scene.

'Jacob, you swine, that's enough. When are you going to learn to take no for an answer?'

'Never!' he ground savagely. 'I'm going to wear you down if it takes the rest of my life.'

'Which it will,' she flung. 'I'm not the fool I once was. Passionate kisses and sweet talk will get you nowhere.

'Then how can I prove I'm sincere?' he grated.

'You can't,' she cried. 'Just get out of my life.' She managed to work her hands between them and pushed with all her strength against his chest. It was like pitting her strength against a brick wall. It was hard and solid and just as immovable.

He caught her hands and held them down at her sides. 'You're mine and you're staying mine. You may as well give in now and let us get on with the job of being married. I've had enough of your melodramatics.'

He sounded bitterly angry and it made Ivory all the more determined not to succumb. 'You can't browbeat me.' Her voice trembled. 'I shall never change my mind.' Her eyes glistened with unshed tears, but she faced him bravely.

Then she turned to look across the harbour. Earlier the tide had been out, revealing an expanse of shiny black mud, but she had been so busy arguing she had not noticed it creeping back in. Now a transformation had taken place.

Side by side they looked out at the estuary beyond the harbour mouth. Gulls circled and screamed overhead. Distant music and singing could still be heard, visitors and residents alike following the Osses and drummers, much as the children had once followed the legendary Pied Piper of Hamlyn.

'We need to talk, Ivory,' he said. 'Let's get out of this place.'

Ivory glanced involuntarily up at the woman, who smiled and nodded as if encouraging her to go with Jacob. She could not know that it was their whole future at stake.

Reluctantly she walked with him away from the harbour across Stile Field towards the War Memorial, not sure that it was a wise decision to leave the comparative safety of the streets.

They walked silently, each occupied with their own thoughts. Jacob's face was grim, a pulse jerking spasmodically in his jaw, and Ivory knew that the time was approaching when she would accuse Jacob of marrying her for all the wrong reasons.

She tried to work out what to say. She did not want to accuse him too harshly, which was odd. But on this beautiful May Day she somehow wanted to keep the peace. She ought never to have said anything. She ought to have enjoyed the day, accepted Jacob's peace-offering, joined in the merriment.

They paused for a rest and Jacob lay down, his hands beneath his head, seeming in no hurry to begin their conversation. He closed his eyes and he looked younger when relaxed, the lines that these last years had riven seeming to fade, his forehead smooth and untroubled, his arrogant nose straight and firm. Thick lashes shadowed his cheeks and his full lips were slightly curved as though some pleasant thoughts were passing through his mind.

He looked very much like the man she had first married and she was overcome with an urge to smother his face with kisses. He was right. She did belong, and the longer she looked at him the stronger grew her desire.

Jacob was her husband, they were still legally wed, and strictly speaking her place was with him. Was she being unnecessarily cruel rejecting him, making it harder for herself? She allowed her eyes to wander down the length of his superbly muscled body. He had never let himself go. He was the fittest man she had ever met.

When she looked back at his face he was watching her, an amused expression in his electric blue eyes. 'What's the verdict?'

She shrugged. 'You're very fit.'

'And virile,' he announced impudently.

She glanced away, annoyed to feel her cheeks grow warm. 'Shall we go on?'

He shrugged and jumped up, pulling her to her feet. They passed Hawker's Cove, where the old lifeboat station still stood, and the coastguard's cottages were still lived in. It was very much like Cornwall must have been a century ago and wove its magic round Ivory until it occurred to her that she never wanted to leave this place. She was being caught by an intangible thread. She ought to make her escape before it was too late. Perhaps Jacob had known this? Perhaps that was why he had brought her to this place?

The path got steeper and hand in hand they

climbed until they reached the Daymark. 'It's like a lighthouse without a light,' she said in surprise.

Jacob smiled. 'That's exactly what it is. 'I believe that at one time it was lit by an oil lamp but now it's no more than a landmark. It welcomes shipping into Padstow and at the same time warns them of the Doom Bar.'

'Doom Bar?' queried Ivory. 'That sounds ominous. What is it?'

'It's brought many sailors to their doom,' he said seriously. 'Across the estuary are several sand bars, but the Doom Bar is the most dangerous. It's covered at high tide. In a storm unwary travellers used to try to shelter in the calm of the estuary, only to find themselves caught on this great bar of sand. Not so many these days, naturally, and the lifeboat does an excellent job, but it's dangerous all the same.'

They sat down on the coarse grass, hugging their knees, looking out across the expanse of shiny blue sea. Ivory had never been in a place that was so incredibly peaceful. It was like being in another world where time stood still.

Far below the sea dashed against the rocks. Gulls screamed. Shags and cormorants stood motionless. It was so warm it could have been summer. 'It's beautiful here,' she said after a while. 'I'm glad you brought me.'

He lay back again, linking his hands beneath his head, looking up at the cloudless blue sky. 'Stepper Point, this is called, and sunset at Stepper is a definite must.'

'I hardly think we'll be here that long,' said Ivory, but he ignored that, continuing:

'It's one of the few remaining unspoilt parts of Cornwall. I think I like it here even better than on Bodmin Moor.'

Which was saying something, she thought, because he loved the moor. He actually enjoyed its bleak desolation. He thought it was beautiful. To Ivory it was remote and unfriendly. She blamed that as much as anything for ruining their marriage.

Perhaps after all, Jacob had done the right thing in bringing her here. Now seemed the right time and the right place to talk about what had gone wrong. Suddenly he pulled her against him and surprisingly, in the crook of his arm, she slept, not waking until she felt something tickle her face. Jacob rested on one elbow, smiling tenderly down, his fingers touching her cheek where he had pushed back a strand of hair.

'Sleepyhead!' he mocked.

'I'm sorry,' she husked. 'I've never done that before.'

'Perhaps it was your sleepless night?'

The taunt was there but Ivory ignored it. 'You should have woken me,' she said, pushing herself up. 'It was very rude of me to go to sleep.'

'I enjoyed looking at you,' he replied. 'But now we must talk. I can be patient no longer. Tell me the reason you think I married you.'

Ivory swallowed a sudden lump in her throat. This was not going to be easy. If he had been in a raging temper she could have flung her accusations at him, but in the tolerant mood he was in how could she? 'Why don't we just call it a day?' she suggested softly. 'Why don't you let me go?'

Jacob snorted. 'You're my wife, Ivory, doesn't that mean anything? You're the only woman I've ever asked to marry me, and I intend keeping you.'

'I don't see the point.' Ivory shook her head, glad of the heavy fall of hair which successfully hid her face. 'Why should two people remain together when they are unhappy?'

'When people are unhappy there has to be a reason. Marriages are only unsuccessful when truths are hidden. If either partner has something to say it should come out in the open, they should not harbour grudges. You've obviously got something against me, Ivory, and it's festering inside you like an untended wound. I want to know what it is. In fact I demand that you tell me. I shan't let you leave this spot until you do.'

Ivory shivered faintly. The sun was sinking lower in the sky, the warmth going out of it. She must have slept longer than she realised.

'I understand,' she began, 'but . . .' She paused. 'Valma said that . . .' Again she stopped. There was no tactful way of saying what needed to be said. She had either to blurt it out or remain silent for ever.

'Valma said what?' he demanded impatiently. 'What has she got to do with it?'

'Valma has everything to do with it,' cried Ivory. 'If it hadn't been for her I'd never have found out. I'd have still been living with you, labouring under the delusion that you loved me.'

For a second she stilled, the harsh lines of his face seemed to be carved out of stone, his icy blue eyes fixed upon her in a gaze so intent that it pinned her to the spot. She was unable to look away and when she spoke again her voice seemed to come from a long way off, it was thin and wavery and sounded entirely unlike her own.

'Valma claims that you only married me to inherit your uncle's fortune,' she went on hurriedly. 'She said that you had a fetish about wealth, that the more you had the more you wanted. She also said that if you weren't married

by your thirty-fifth birthday Giles would inherit—and no way did you want that. And since
she was on a cruise at that time you married the
first gullible girl you met—who happened to be
me!' She paused for breath, having been unable
to stop once she had started.

Jacob's face was a picture of incredulity. 'And
you believed her?'

'Naturally,' exclaimed Ivory. 'Everything
began to make sense. I'd never been able to
understand exactly why you asked me to marry
you. I mean, I'm not even in your league, I never
have been, I never will be. You're seventeen
years older than me. It just doesn't add up.'

'Then why did you marry me?' he grated.

'I was flattered. At first I thought I loved you,
but I soon outgrew that.'

'When you met Giles!' The words came thickly
from deep in his throat. 'But that's another story.
Tell me, now you know him, do you think I did
the right thing? Do you reckon Giles would have
got through my uncle's inheritance with no more
compunction than a child spending its pocket
money on sweets?'

Ivory knew he would have done. She had
learned enough about Jacob's half-brother to
realise that money slid through his fingers like
water. No matter how much he had he would
always spend it. Never once thinking about
tomorrow, always living for today.

There had been more than one occasion when
he had asked her for money, thinking she had
easy access to Jacob's bank account, and although
she had been tempted, knowing that some of it
should belong to him, she had always refused.

But she was reluctant to admit this to Jacob. 'I
think it might have made a difference to him,' she

said instead. 'So far as I can see he's never had
the chance to prove himself.'

'God, Ivory, how can you think such a thing?
Giles is an empty-headed little fool. He'll never
make a go of anything, not until he learns sense
and grows up. If he'd had that money it would
have all gone by now—and you know it. So why
the hell are you sticking up for him? I suppose it
means that you still love him?'

'Someone has to stand by him,' cried Ivory,
ignoring this last gibe. 'It appears to me that
you've always had a down on him and it's given
him an inferiority complex.'

'Inferiority complex be damned,' grated Jacob.
'He was as high as a kite when he took you from
me. He lapped it up, losing no opportunity at all
to tell me what a fantastic lover you were.' He
spat the word out in disgust. 'I sometimes think I
need my head examining wanting you back after
you've been sullied by that—scum!'

Ivory flinched at the venom in his tone. 'I see
you've not denied that that was the reason you
married me?'

His lips firmed. 'There's no point, is there? If
you really believe it, it would be foolhardy to
insist you continue to live with me as my wife. I
don't think I could stand making love to a woman
who despises me.'

Ivory swallowed painfully. She felt as though
her heart had been slashed in two. She had, in the
beginning, hated Jacob for what he had done,
only afterwards discovering that her love was a
far stronger emotion. But if Jacob did not love
her, and she had no reason to believe that he did,
then he was right. There was no point in going
on.

She jumped up and with a brightness she was

far from feeling said, 'So that's that. When are we going back to London, tomorrow? I see no point in prolonging the agony.'

'If that's what you want.' His expression was enigmatic.

'It is,' she said firmly.

They began walking and the silence between them was unbearable. The sky, which had been clear all day now had a few wispy clouds drifting across. The sun had transformed the sea to a molten gold, turning to a deeper shade as it slowly and visibly sank.

Even after it had disappeared the sky glowed for a long time, giving the impression that a fire raged somewhere out of sight. The golds turned to red, the clouds changed shape, became tinged with gold and red, yellow and black, sky and sea merging in a kaleidoscope of colour.

Ivory felt moved by the beauty of the scene and wished she could share her appreciation with Jacob. But one look at his face and she knew he was blind to all about him.

He looked like a man who had lost everything. There was even a droop to his shoulders which was unusual because Jacob was a man who always stood upright, physically and mentally. She guessed that never before had he gambled and lost.

When they got back into Padstow it was dark and the May Day festivities had almost finished. As they passed through, the Old Oss did a dance round the maypole before finally being stabled at the Golden Lion. It was the end to what could have been a happy day.

That night Jacob slept in one of the spare rooms. As Ivory lay in the big double bed she felt cheated. Jacob had cheated her. He had cheated her out of her happiness. At a time when she should have been going out with her friends he had persuaded her to marry him, with such tragic consequences that she had felt an old woman before she was twenty.

She wondered what the future held in store. Would Jacob divorce her? Was that what he wanted, or was it his intention to keep her tied to him? Did he mean to punish her in this way? It was an unfortunate state of affairs and she could not see where it would end.

It was a relief when they were back in London, but although she had expected him to take her to her aunt's he insisted that she remain at his apartment.

'You still have a duty to perform,' he said coldly. 'Naturally, we shall sleep in separate rooms.' And that was as much as he said to her.

The only times they made conversation were when he brought guests back for dinner. Ivory was then expected to behave as though nothing at all was wrong. Jacob became a Jekyll and Hyde character. In front of his colleagues he was the doting loving husband and it sickened her. How she would love to tell them that the moment the door closed behind them he ignored her.

Not that she would have wanted it any other way. All she wanted to do was leave him. She hated living in the same apartment yet leading totally separate lives. It made no sense. He was exacting his pound of flesh, but at what price?

Long week followed long week and Ivory began to wonder where it would all end. She had never been more unhappy in her life. Jacob had issued Mrs Humphrey with instructions to see that Ivory ate proper meals, and she did so simply because there was no point in making herself ill. To keep up with Jacob's exacting treatment she needed all her strength.

Once a week she visited her aunt, but was careful not to let Eleanor see that there was anything wrong. The woman consistently enquired why Jacob never accompanied her, and Ivory always insisted that he was working himself so hard that she did not see much of him herself.

Then one day Valma turned up. It was early evening and Ivory was expecting Jacob home from work. Humphrey had gone. Ivory had changed as she always did for dinner whether they had visitors or not, her face carefully made up to disguise the pallor of her cheeks, the heavy shadows beneath her eyes.

When she opened the door there was nothing about her to suggest that there was anything wrong with their marriage. Superficially she looked a contented woman. Without waiting to be invited Valma stepped into the room. 'Where's Jacob?' she enquired, looking around. 'He knows the show starts at seven-thirty.'

Ivory eyed Valma disdainfully, hating all that this woman stood for. She wore a jersey lurex dress that clung sensuously to her voluptuous curves. A silver-fox stole was draped elegantly about her shoulders, her blonde hair coiled on top of her head revealing the long slender length of her neck, about which was clasped a diamond necklace.

Ivory wondered whether Jacob had brought her any of these expensive accessories, feeling a raging jealousy, wishing he had arranged to meet the woman elsewhere. It was like sticking a knife into an already open wound.

Unable to keep the open hostility from her voice she said, 'As far as I know he's still working. He never does let me know what time he'll be in unless he's bringing someone back with him.'

Valma smiled contentedly, 'Jacob always lets me know what he's doing. The moment he knew I was over he phoned me and suggested we have an evening out.'

'How nice.' Ivory did not believe her. If the truth was known it was probably Valma who had telephoned Jacob.

'But then, of course,' purred Valma, 'I think I'd be correct in saying that I know him better than you.'

'I've no doubt.' Ivory's voice was terse and she turned her back, unable to look at this feline woman any longer.

'I'll have a drink while I'm waiting.' Valma crossed to the cupboard where Jacob always kept a plentiful supply, pouring herself a generous measure of gin to which she added just a dash of soda water.

'If you'll excuse me,' said Ivory, 'I have things to do in the kitchen. Were you planning to eat here?' Only natural courtesy made her ask, there was no way she wanted Valma to join them.

The woman shook her head. 'We should have been gone ten minutes ago. I think I'll phone him.'

She was on the telephone for no more than a minute, then she slammed the receiver down and turned on Ivory viciously. 'Jacob's not the same since he married you. All he seems to want to do is work. He was never like that. He always had time for me. Now he has the nerve to say he can't make it, that something cropped up at the last minute. He'd never have let that happen before. I think he's pushing himself too far. I think he's drowning his sorrows in work.'

Ivory glared. 'We both know why he married me. You made sure of that.'

'Then why,' queried Valma bitterly, 'are you still here? Have you no pride?'

'I'm here,' she smiled quietly, 'because that is what Jacob wants. He knows I've discovered the reason he chose me.' It pleased her to see the sudden shock on Valma's face. 'Oh yes, I told him what you'd said, but he insisted that my place is with him. I don't know why you're wasting your time running around after him.'

The colour flooded Valma's hard face, and then drained, leaving her as white as paper. 'Are you trying to tell me that Jacob intends keeping up this ridiculous charade?'

Ivory inclined her head, saying smoothly, 'I think he happens to believe in the *for better or for worse* vows that he took. I'm afraid, Valma, that if you thought I would insist on a divorce once I knew why he had married me then you're mistaken. But it's Jacob's idea, not mine, I don't mind telling you that. And when a man insists his wife stays with him it can mean only one thing— that he loves her.'

Her heart hammered as she uttered the lie, but it did her good to see the uncertainty on Valma's face. It was the first time she had seen this other woman unsure of herself.

'Jacob loves me,' Valma insisted, but without the confidence that normally accompanied her words.

'If Jacob loved you,' said Ivory, 'he would never have married me. And since he can't even be bothered to take time off from work when you've flown over purposely from the States, I think that speaks for itself. I love Jacob very much and there is no way I intend losing him to you. I'm afraid you've had a wasted journey.'

Valma stared at her for several long seconds before finishing her drink in a couple of

swallows, and then stalking on her inevitable high
heels out of the apartment. 'This isn't the last
you've heard of this,' she flung over her shoulder.

When she had gone Ivory sank down on to the
chesterfield. It had taken courage to speak to Valma
in that way, but she was glad she had done it. She
felt a whole lot better. She refused to think what
Jacob might say when he heard how she had spoken
to his girlfriend, but whatever it was worth it. The
deflated look on Valma's face was something she
would remember for a long time.

She ate a solitary dinner and played a new
James Last L.P. that she had bought that
afternoon, and then, when there was still no sign
of Jacob, went to bed. For a long time she lay
awake listening for him, wondering whether
Valma had gone to his office, whether in fact they
were out together.

It felt as though a clawed hand clutched her
stomach and resolutely she pushed them from her
mind. But no matter how she tried to think of
something else her thoughts always returned to
Jacob and Valma.

It was after one when she heard him enter the
apartment. He came charging into her room,
snapping on the light, towering at the end of the bed.

Although she had instinctively closed her eyes
against the sudden brightness she was aware of
the rage that trembled within him. The very room
seemed to vibrate with his anger, and she could not
think what had put him in this frame of mind.

'I want to know what you've been saying to
Valma,' he demanded.

The unexpectedness of his words made Ivory's
eyes pop open. 'I've said nothing,' she replied,
'nothing that I'm ashamed of. If she's been
blackening my character it's probably because she

was annoyed that you were working tonight when you'd promised to take her out.'

'Valma would never lie,' said Jacob crossly.

Ivory privately thought he was a fool to believe that, but nevertheless said calmly, 'Suppose you tell me what it is I'm supposed to have said, and I'll tell you whether it's the truth.'

'I don't need to,' he snarled. 'There's no reason for Valma to lie.'

Ivory sighed. 'Since I haven't the slightest idea what you are talking about, there's nothing I can say.' She was becoming irritated by his manner. 'And now, Jacob, I'd like to go to sleep, if you don't mind. I'm very tired.'

'And so am I,' he yelled, 'tired of this whole stupid affair. Do you deny telling Valma that she had no right to see me now that I'm married?'

Ivory shrugged. 'I don't recall using those exact words, but I suppose that is something like what I said.'

'And what right have you to decree who should or should not be my friends?' he demanded. There was an ugly flush beneath his skin and his blue eyes had a steely sheen. He was a daunting man at the best of times. At this moment, though, Ivory felt extremely fragile. She was at his mercy and he looked angry enough to do anything.

'When Valma comes here and gloats over the fact that she is spending the evening with my husband there is no way that I can sit quietly and take it,' she said.

'In a marriage as disastrous as ours,' returned Jacob impatiently, 'the only way I can keep sane is by going out with another woman.'

Ivory cringed at the bitterness in his tone. 'Thanks for nothing.' Her voice was high, unlike her usual well-modulated tones. 'If it's other

women you want why are you keeping me here?
Why don't you let me go then you can have half a
dozen at a time for all I care.'

'Are you forgetting,' asked Jacob, 'that you
have a debt to pay?'

'I haven't forgotten,' retorted Ivory bitterly.
'Perhaps you'd like to tell me how many years
you think it will take? I used to think that you
were charging for my services, but since we now
have separate rooms it can hardly be that. I can't
see that you're getting anything at all out of this
relationship. I know I'm not. It's a living hell,
and I rue the day I met you.' She pulled the
sheets about her shoulders and buried her face in
the pillow. 'Good night, Jacob.'

But she was not to get any peace. Angrily he
snatched the sheets from her. She wore nothing
more than a short silk nightdress. It was
transparent and had cost the earth. It was one
that he had selected himself in the early days of
their marriage.

His eyes flickered over it, hunger in their
depths, and before she knew what was happening
Ivory found him bearing down on top of her. Her
heart-beats quickened as his eager hands tore at
the flimsy material.

His hot lips took possession of her mouth.
There was an urgency about him that she had
never experienced before. She felt afraid and
tried to beat him off, but the attempt was futile, it
made no difference, her blows slid off him like
water off a duck's back.

When he suddenly pushed himself away Ivory
thought for one moment that he had changed his
mind. But far from it. He ripped off his shirt, pop-
ping buttons as he did so, unzipping his trousers
and stepping out of them in one fluid movement.

And then he was on top of her again. It could
have been rape had Ivory not been so responsive.
All the feelings she had bottled up over these last
weeks exploded into a frenzy of emotion. Her
body felt as though it was about to burst, fires
raging within her, tremors taking hold of each
and every limb.

Jacob's lips were feverish on her face, demanding, possessing. There was no gentleness about
him. He was consumed by a passion greater than
himself. There was no stopping him now.

His hands bruised her body as they intimately
explored. He slid down and took her breasts one by
one into his mouth, biting and teasing until her
nipples were hard and swollen, and she throbbed
and ached with a longing that destroyed her.

Long before the final moment of loving came
Ivory was arching herself towards him, ready and
eager to accept all that he wanted to give. He
made love more violently than she had ever
remembered, and when it was over fell heavily at
her side. Both their bodies were damp with
perspiration. Ivory felt completely bereft.

He had transported her into a world of the
senses that she would never forget. If it was the
last time Jacob ever made love to her then it was
also the most beautiful. He had ravaged her soul,
he had demanded, and got, a complete response,
and he had given to her every part of himself.

When at length he finally moved he groaned,
and propping himself up on one elbow looked
down into her face. All the aggression had gone
out of him. He looked oddly humble. 'I'm sorry,
Ivory, I shouldn't have done that. Please forgive
me. I suppose now you hate me even more?'

'I don't hate you, Jacob.' Ivory felt that the
moment for truth had come. It was impossible to

go on hiding her fears. No matter what the consequences were she wanted Jacob to know how she felt. What had just happened meant more to her than anything in her life.

'I love you.' She said the words slowly and carefully, her stomach tightening as she looked into his eyes. She wanted to see exactly what reaction her confession drew. Certainly what she did not expect was for his face to crumple with an emotion that seemed to wrack his body.

With a cry of sheer anguish he crushed her to him. She felt his hair-roughened skin beneath her naked breasts, the pounding of his heart. It had never before been so loud or insistent and she wondered. Tilting back her head she looked into his eyes. 'Tell me, Jacob,' she implored softly, 'am I being a fool?'

He groaned hoarsely. 'It's what I've been waiting for you to say ever since the day I married you. How long have you known?'

She shook her head weakly. 'Always, I think. When I found out why you had married me it really crucified me. I couldn't believe that you would do such a thing. I wanted to hate you, but I couldn't. I continually told myself what a despot you were but it didn't work. I loved you. It was as simple as that.'

'I wish you'd told me,' he said. 'It would have saved all this agony. I've loved you desperately ever since the day I first met you. I've waited and waited for the day that you would return my love.'

Ivory felt her breath catch in her throat. 'I didn't know you—loved me.'

'But of course.' He looked at her as though she was insane. 'I've always loved you, Ivory. Wasn't that clear?'

She shook her head. 'You never told me.'

'Did I have to? Wasn't it obvious? Why else would I have showered you with gifts? I wanted to give you the whole world. It was my way of telling you how I felt. I thought you knew.'

She moaned and pressed herself against him, offering her lips to his, and the sweetness of his kiss sent fresh quivers of emotion through her, and before she knew it Jacob was making love to her all over again.

'I'm glad we've sorted it out, Jacob,' she said at length. 'It was agony living with you, loving you, but being treated as though I meant no more to you than Humphrey.'

'My darling, it hurt me more than it hurt you. You don't know how many times I've wanted to take you into my arms, how many times I've got as far as your bedroom door and then turned away. It's been the hardest battle of my life.'

'I'm sorry,' she said quietly, 'and if it will help, there have been times when I wanted to come to you too.'

'I thought you loved Giles,' he muttered thickly. 'Please tell me he never meant anything to you.'

Ivory took his face between her hands. 'I can tell you that in all honesty, Jacob. Giles has done nothing more than kiss me. I used him, just as I thought you were using me. He enjoyed playing the part. I had no idea, though, that he had kept it up all this while. I've only seen him a few times.

'Thank God,' he breathed fervently. 'It was the hardest decision I have ever had to make, letting you go. The thought of Giles making love to you sickened me. I felt physically ill. I really thought you had decided I was too old and because I wanted you to be happy, more than anything else, more than my own happiness, I decided I had no right to stand in your way.'

Ivory felt very humble and her eyes were moist as she looked into his face. How much he had suffered—and all because he had put her before himself. 'I'm sorry,' she whispered.

'Don't be, it's over, it's finished.' There was still pain on his face. 'But I don't mind telling you now that it's a wonder I never killed Giles. I went after him more than once, only common sense and the thought that I might be hurting you in the process, stopping me.'

He shuddered and Ivory held him in her arms, crying quietly inside, wondering how they could have both been so blind.

'To keep the records straight,' he said at length, 'I didn't use you. I know what Valma said, and it was true that if I had not married my uncle's fortune would have gone to Giles, but that wasn't the reason. It was maybe the reason why I rushed you into it—but I knew you were the girl I wanted to marry one day anyway. Did you really think I was as avaricious as all that?'

'I didn't want to believe it,' she said softly. 'But what else could I think?'

He smiled sadly. 'I've put the money into a trust fund for Giles. He will get it when he's twenty-five. I hope by then he will have learned some sense.'

'Oh, Jacob!' exclaimed Ivory. 'I'm sorry I ever doubted you.'

'Don't be,' he said. 'There was no way that you could know whether Valma was speaking the truth, unless you had asked me. Why didn't you?'

She grimaced wryly. 'It was too humiliating. It meant admitting that I'd been taken in. I was afraid I'd show my own feelings.'

'As a matter of fact,' he said, 'Valma only told you half the tale. She knew I had done it for Giles's own good, but she was jealous of you. It grieved her that I'd married behind her back.'

'Was she expecting you to marry her?'

He grinned. 'She was waiting for me to ask, then would have taken great delight in saying no. It would never have worked. We were far too familiar for that. I've known her since she was about sixteen and have never been under any delusions as to the sort of woman she is. I'm afraid I've been guilty of using her to get at you.'

'Then we're quits,' said Ivory gently.

'I'll never hurt you again,' he promised, 'you're too precious to me. God, I was so angry with myself that day I discovered you hadn't been eating. I knew I was responsible.'

'There's a chance you might have to be responsible for someone else in the near future,' she ventured shyly.

A quick frown darkened his handsome brow.

'Your son,' said Ivory quickly.

His frown changed to a smile. 'Ivory, is that true? Are you really pregnant? Oh, God, I hope I haven't hurt you. You should have told me. You should have stopped me.'

She shook her head and smiled. 'How could I when I've wanted you for so long? But I'm glad you're pleased. It's been agony keeping it to myself.'

'You're sure it's going to be a boy?'

'Oh, yes.' Ivory nodded vigorously. 'With blue eyes and black hair, and a smile like his father.'

'And our next will be a girl, like you. Just like you, my sweet Ivory. Remind me to tell you every single day for the rest of my life that I love you.' He pulled her to him, but this time he was more gentle, mindful of the baby developing inside her.

Ivory felt content. Her months of heartache were over. There was no doubt in her mind now of their future happiness.

MARCH 85 (UK) HARDBACK TITLES

—— ROMANCE ——

SOUTHERN SUNSHINE Gloria Bevan	0 263 10774 4
CAPRICORN MAN Jacqueline Gilbert	0 263 10775 2
BUSHRANGER'S MOUNTAIN Victoria Gordon	0 263 10776 0
BIG SUR Elizabeth Graham	0 263 10777 9
THE OBJECT OF THE GAME Vanessa James	0 263 10778 7
TAKEN OVER Penny Jordan	0 263 10779 5
HOSTAGE Madeleine Ker	0 263 10780 9
ALMOST A BRIDE Maura McGiveny	0 263 10781 7
DARK OBSESSION Valerie Marsh	0 263 10782 5
A COMPELLING FORCE Margaret Mayo	0 263 10783 3
TRUST IN TOMORROW Carole Mortimer	0 263 10784 1
MODEL OF DECEPTION Margaret Pargeter	0 263 10785 X
THE IRON HEART Edwina Shore	0 263 10786 8
DOUBLE DECEPTION Kay Thorpe	0 263 10787 6
EAGLE'S RIDGE Margaret Way	0 263 10788 4
A ROOTED SORROW Nicola West	0 263 10789 2

MASQUERADE HISTORICAL ROMANCE

THE RIVER OF TIME Dinah Dean	0 263 10814 7
BEWARE THE CONQUEROR Anne Herries	0 263 10815 5

DOCTOR NURSE ROMANCE

A SURGEON CALLS Hazel Fisher	0 263 10796 5
PATIENCE AND DR PRITCHARD Lilian Darcy	0 263 10797 3

LARGE PRINT

AN ELUSIVE DESIRE Anne Mather	0 263 10818 X
CLOUDED RAPTURE Margaret Pargeter	0 263 10819 8
JILTED Sally Wentworth	0 263 10820 1

APRIL 85 (UK) HARDBACK TITLES

——— ROMANCE ———

Time of Change *Rosalind Cowdray*	0 263 10798 1
Don't Play Games *Emma Darcy*	0 263 10799 X
A World of Difference *Sandra Field*	0 263 10800 7
Age of Consent *Victoria Gordon*	0 263 10801 5
Outcast Lovers *Sarah Holland*	0 263 10802 3
Time Fuse *Penny Jordan*	0 263 10803 1
Man Hunt *Charlotte Lamb*	0 263 10804 X
Acapulco Moonlight *Marjorie Lewty*	0 263 10805 8
Eclipse of the Heart *Mary Lyons*	0 263 10806 6
Dreams to Keep *Leigh Michaels*	0 263 10807 4
Lovers in the Afternoon *Carole Mortimer*	0 263 10808 2
Dare to Trust *Anne McAllister*	0 263 10809 0
Impasse *Margaret Pargeter*	0 263 10810 4
Inherit the Storm *Valerie Parv*	0 263 10811 2
Pelangi Haven *Karen van der Zee*	0 263 10812 0
A Secret Pleasure *Flora Kidd*	0 263 10813 9

MASQUERADE HISTORICAL ROMANCE

Black Ravenswood *Valentina Luellen*	0 263 10849 X
Spaniard's Haven *Lynne Brooks*	0 263 10850 3

DOCTOR NURSE ROMANCE

Dr Delisle's Inheritance *Sarah Franklin*	0 263 10816 3
Bachelor of Hearts *Leonie Craig*	0 263 10817 1

LARGE PRINT

Gallant Antagonist *Jessica Steele*	0 263 10821 X
Forbidden Wine *Lynsey Stevens*	0 263 10822 8
No Alternative *Margaret Way*	0 263 10823 6